As they approached the midway point of the crossing Avery stopped dead. Katsuko barrelled straight into the back of him.

'What?'

He spun around. They were dead centre. Exactly where he wanted to be.

A few eyebrows rose from the people who sidestepped around them.

'What are you doing? Are you crazy? We need to cross before the lights change.'

Katsuko's head was darting from side to side. Time was running out.

But not for Avery.

He caught her head between both his hands. Her hair shone in the neon light and her eyes sparkled. '*This* is what I'm doing,' he said as he bent down and caught her perfect strawberry lips in his.

He felt her breath catch. But she was only rigid for the tiniest moment. One second later her body relaxed against his. Her lips were soft, pliable, and seemed as if they were moulded just for his. His hands moved from her cheeks and tangled through her silky-soft hair. He could smell her. He could smell the perfume she was wearing, the shampoo in her hair and the strawberry from her lip gloss. He'd be happy if he could stay there all night, just inhaling her.

Her hands moved up to his shoulders, her fingers brushing against the skin at the side of his neck.

Reaction. That was just what he needed. Right in the middle of the busiest crossing in the world.

Dear Reader,

I absolutely *loved* writing this story set in Tokyo. It gave me a chance to learn about a new country and culture and also gave me the opportunity to look at the point of view of foreign personnel based there.

My US Air Force base is fictional, but there *are* a number of real US Air Force bases in Japan. I might have stolen a little bit of information from them all!

My heroine, Katsuko, is of mixed race: half-Japanese and half-African-American. Her nickname in Japanese is 'firecracker', and although professionally it might suit her, on a personal level she's a lot less confident than she seems.

It takes a good man like my hero, newcomer Captain Avery Flynn, to recognise the signs and help build my heroine's confidence. He has issues of his own, but spending time with Katsuko helps him realise that he's met someone worth taking a chance on.

I love to hear from readers. Please feel free to contact me via my website, scarlet-wilson.com, or via Facebook or Twitter.

Happy reading!

Love,

Scarlet x

ONE KISS IN TOKYO...

BY

SCARLET WILSON

Published in Great Britain 2016
By Mills & Boon, an imprint of HarperCollins*Publishers*
1 London Bridge Street, London, SE1 9GF

ISBN: 978-0-263-06553-4

Our policy is to use papers that are natural, renewable and recyclable products and made from wood grown in sustainable forests. The logging and manufacturing processes conform to the legal environmental regulations of the country of origin.

Printed and bound in Great Britain
by CPI Antony Rowe, Chippenham, Wiltshire

Scarlet Wilson wrote her first story aged eight and has never stopped. She's worked in the health service for twenty years, trained as a nurse and a health visitor. Scarlet now works in public health and lives on the West Coast of Scotland with her fiancé and their two sons. Writing medical romances and contemporary romances is a dream come true for her.

Books by Scarlet Wilson

Mills & Boon Medical Romance

Midwives On-Call at Christmas
A Touch of Christmas Magic

Christmas with the Maverick Millionaire
The Doctor She Left Behind
The Doctor's Baby Secret

Mills & Boon Cherish

Tycoons in a Million
Holiday with the Millionaire
A Baby to Save Their Marriage

The Vineyards of Calanetti
His Lost-and-Found Bride

Visit the Author Profile page at millsandboon.co.uk for more titles.

This book is dedicated with thanks to Kay Thomas—
a fellow author—and her son,
who was good enough to help me with my Japanese!

Praise for
Scarlet Wilson

'The book is filled with high-strung emotions, engaging dialogue, breathtaking descriptions and characters you just cannot help but love. With the magic of Christmas as a bonus, you won't be disappointed with this story!'

—*Goodreads* on
A Touch of Christmas Magic

'*200 Harley Street: Girl from the Red Carpet* is a fast-paced and feel-good medical romance that sparkles with red-hot sensuality, mesmerising emotion and intense passion.'

—*Goodreads*

'I am totally addicted to this author's books. Not once have I picked up a book by her and felt disappointed or let down. She creates intense, perfect characters with so many amazing levels of emotion it blows my mind time and time again.'

—*Contemporary Romance Reviews* on
Tempted by Her Boss

CHAPTER ONE

THE NOISE HAD CHANGED. The steady drone of the engines had taken on a new pitch. Avery lifted his hat from over his eyes and sat up a little. Every bone in his body ached; muscles he hadn't even known he had were protesting. Three plane journeys over twelve hours would do that to a man. It didn't help that he'd been on duty for twenty-four hours before that.

He'd expected to have a few days' rest before shipping out to Italy from Utah. But plans in the US Air Force often came unstuck.

His orders had changed overnight. A fellow physician who'd been scheduled to come to Japan had been struck down with a mystery illness. So, instead of flying over the boot-shaped coast of Italy, he found himself looking at the emerging coastline of Japan. The change of noise was due to the flaps moving and wheels coming down on the aircraft. His stomach growled loudly and the serviceman sitting next to him gave him a smile and passed over a packet of crisps. They weren't flying on a commercial jet—there were no air hostesses, no bar and no food. They were flying on a military jet and it wasn't exactly built for comfort. Avery couldn't wait to find his accommodation and get his head down for a few hours. Sleep was all he cared about right now.

The plane landed with a bump. He pulled open the packet of crisps and started eating—the quicker he ate the sooner he would get to sleep. The jet took a few minutes to taxi to a halt. The rest of the servicemen were grabbing their packs, ready to disembark.

Avery kept looking outside, trying to get a better feel for the base. It housed nineteen thousand servicemen and servicewomen and contained one of the biggest military hospitals. Set in the outskirts of Tokyo, the base was a home away from home. Most of the staff stayed on-site. There were stores, cafés, schools for the kids, places of worship and even a golf course. The base had been here since the end of the Second World War.

He waited until the rest of the servicemen disembarked before finally grabbing his backpack and walking down the steps of the plane.

The warm air hit him straight away. The base was situated on the coast, and the air was muggy. He could see the metropolis of Tokyo stretching in front of him. He smiled. A whole world he'd never experienced.

He was kind of excited. He'd been stationed in a range of bases all around the world. Normally, he spent a little time finding about where he'd be stationed. Europe. The Middle East. And numerous places around the US. This time around he hadn't had a chance. He'd no idea what he'd find at Okatu.

He followed the rest of the servicemen into the main hangar. Transfer between bases always took a little paperwork. A few were already heading towards the housing department.

Avery sighed and completed his obligatory paperwork and picked up the information sheet on the base. His stomach growled again. There was no way he could sleep until he'd eaten. It made more sense to find something to eat first, then come back and speak to the housing officer to find out where he'd be staying.

He walked out of the building, glanced at his sheet and turned left. He took things slowly, trying to shake off all the aches and pains of travel. The base was huge and during the stroll he passed an elementary school, a middle school, a gymnasium, the officers' club, a travel centre, a few shops and a library. It was a fifteen-minute walk before the ten-year-old hospital appeared before him.

There it was. The buzz. The tickle. That crazy little sensation he felt whenever he saw somewhere new. The William Bates Memorial Hospital was named after an aviator hero from the First World War. It had one hundred and fifty beds, an ER, four theatres, an ICU, a mother-and-infant care centre, a neonatal intensive care unit, a medical ward, a surgical ward and a mental health inpatient facility. He loved hospitals like this. Most surgeons liked to specialise in one area. The military gave surgeons that opportunity too—there were a few specialists already here. But Avery had never just wanted to work in one area. He liked variety—and here he would get it.

He started to walk towards the main entrance to the hospital, then changed his mind, turning right and heading towards the ER. He may as well get a look around the place.

The glass doors slid open just as a siren started to sound. He looked around. The main reception area was empty. Where was everyone?

It didn't take long to find out. Someone came running towards him, making the doors ahead slide open. He took a quick glance and kept walking down the corridor.

The ER was set up like many he'd worked in before. Cubicles with curtains, some side rooms, a treatment room and a room with around ten people standing outside. Resus, the most important room in the ER.

A Japanese orderly rushed past, pushing a wheelchair.

He threw Avery a second glance, looking him up and down. 'You work here?'

He nodded and waved his ID. 'From tomorrow. Captain Avery Flynn. I'm a doctor.' He was relieved the man had spoken to him in English. He didn't know a word of Japanese and he wasn't sure if it was going to be a problem. Most military bases didn't just serve their own personnel. Often they took cases from the surrounding areas. Having no grasp of the language could prove a problem.

The man gave him a nod. 'No time for introductions. We're expecting seven.'

He disappeared quicker than a cartoon character. Seven what? wondered Avery. 'Oof!'

A force hit him from behind, knocking him clean off his feet and onto the floor. He barely had time to put out his hands to break his fall.

'Get out of the way' came the sharp voice.

All he could see was feet. Lots of feet, crammed into the resus room. He pushed himself up and shrugged off his backpack. If he was needed, he was needed.

A hand grabbed him from behind and a male nurse grinned at him. 'Hey, you must be new. Falling for the nurses already?'

Avery blinked as he dumped his jacket next to his backpack and flashed his ID. 'What...? Who was that?'

The guy hadn't stopped smiling. *'Faiyakuraka.'*

'What?' Avery couldn't quite make sense of the word.

The guy tapped him on the shoulder. 'It's Japanese for firecracker. But you can only call her that once you know her well. For you, it'll be Katsuko.' Then he shook his head. 'Actually, let's try to keep you safe. Just call her First Lieutenant Williams.' He moved forward. 'Now, let's see if you're any good or not.' And with that, he disappeared into the scrum in front of them.

It was difficult to tell who was who. These people

weren't in regular military uniforms. The majority of them wore the usual garb for an ER—pale green scrubs. He had no idea who was a nurse, a doctor or an aerospace medical technician.

'I need an airway. I need an airway now!' came the shout.

Avery shouldered his way in.

It brought everything into focus. That, he could do.

He put up his hand. 'I'll do it.' A few heads turned at the unfamiliar voice and a little space appeared in the crowd.

The woman who had sent him flying had her short dark hair leaning over the patient. Her head shot up and her eyes narrowed. She had the darkest brown eyes he'd ever seen.

'Who are you?'

Blood. Everywhere. All over the chest of a young child. His reactions were instant. Now he understood the clamour around the bed. Hands were everywhere, pressing on the little chest, trying to stem the flow.

The woman was right. This young patient needed an airway now.

The large penetrating wound—a spear of some kind through the chest—told him everything he needed to know.

He moved to the top of the bed and nudged her out of his way. Or, at least, he tried to.

Her hips stayed firmly in place. 'Who are you?' She was practically growling at him.

He glanced at the nearby trolley, opening the first few drawers until he found what he needed. 'Do we have IV access?' he asked a nurse to his left.

'Just,' she said promptly.

A small, firm hand closed over his. He turned around. The woman who'd sent him flying was just about in his face. Her dark brown eyes could have swallowed him up. She spoke so quietly he was sure no one else could hear. 'I'm not going to ask you again.' She gave a squeeze over his hand—and this time her grip was like iron. 'I'm just going to break your hand.'

He lifted his ID and slid it between both their faces. 'Let me do my job. We've got six months to fight with each other.'

She was small, obviously of Japanese descent but her skin was slightly darker than he would have expected. Her hair was poker straight, cut very short at the nape of her neck but becoming longer down past her ears. From straight on it looked like a bob. A smart cut for a nurse, short enough to be off her collar but not long enough to need tying up every day.

There seemed to be something about her. A presence. She was like a cannonball. People paid attention to her even though she couldn't be the highest-ranking person in the room. Far from it, in fact. She only looked in her mid-twenties.

Firecracker? He couldn't remember what the Japanese word was but somehow the nickname suited her. It seemed to sum her up perfectly.

It was obvious that in this room people respected her. He liked that. He liked that she was direct and efficient at her job.

Her eyes shifted and focused on the ID. She turned without a word and started shouting orders at others in the room. 'Get an IV run through.' She glanced at the endotracheal tube in the hand of her colleague. 'I think we'll need something smaller.'

Perfect. A nurse he could work with. All air force and military nurses and personnel were efficient and well trained. But he always worked best with those who could think ahead and weren't afraid to voice their opinion. He had a sneaky suspicion that Katsuko—was that her name?—would never be afraid to voice her opinion.

Avery tried to ignore the bedlam around him. He tried to

cut out the noise. There were two trolleys in the resus room and another team was working on another patient. They were moving like clockwork, performing cardiac massage.

He moved swiftly. 'Any other doctors in here?'

'Two are up on the helipad. They haven't even managed to get the patient down yet.' She pressed her lips together. 'Blake won't give up on the other kid. Not until he's tried everything.'

The doctor attending to the little boy on the other trolley. Blake Anderson. The guy he was supposed to report to tomorrow. The scene on the other trolley was disheartening and he didn't feel the urge to introduce himself right now. If he didn't pay attention to the kid directly in front of him, he might end up resuscitating him too.

Avery took a breath and held out his hand. The area around this little boy's neck and chest was swelling, a reaction to the severe injury that could compromise his airway. His sallow skin was losing its natural colour rapidly. A nurse was poised next to the IV meds, awaiting his instructions. He gave them quickly. Something for pain control. Something to sedate the boy and steroids to reduce the swelling and allow him to intubate. Airway first. Everything else later.

The nurse nodded and inserted the drugs into the IV cannula on the inside of the kid's elbow.

'ET tube.' Avery held out his hand, bending down at the top of the trolley and tilting the little boy's head. 'Do we have his name?'

'Mahito. His name is Mahito.' The firecracker nurse was watching his every move.

'Mahito, I've given you something for the pain and something to relax you. I'm going to have to slide a tube down your throat. Don't panic. We'll take good care of you.' It didn't matter that the little Japanese boy might not understand a word of English, or his Ohio accent.

He'd done this a hundred times before and he'd do it a hundred times again.

He gave Katsuko a few seconds as she translated his words rapidly. The little boy was barely conscious. He probably had no awareness of what was going on right now and that wasn't a bad thing.

He tilted the little boy's head back, lifting his jaw and sliding the silver laryngoscope into place. He could barely visualise the cords—if he waited any longer he'd probably have to do an emergency tracheotomy—but thankfully he had time to slide the thin blue ET tube into place and inflate the cuff. It took less than four seconds to secure the airway. He attached the bag to the end of the tube and let the nurse take over.

With the airway secure he could now take a few minutes to assess the situation properly. 'We're going to need to take him to Theatre. Can I get a portable chest X-ray?'

A woman in a blue tunic stepped forward, pushing the machine towards them. She'd been waiting for his signal. Like in most military hospitals, radiographers were always available in the ER.

A heavy lead-lined apron was dropped over his head. He didn't even question where it had come from. A few people stepped from the room for a second.

'Done,' said the radiographer.

She glanced back at Avery. He could see the question on her face. 'Avery Flynn. I officially start tomorrow.'

Satisfied with his answer, she gave a nod. 'Dr Flynn, I'll have your X-ray in a few minutes.'

Avery nodded. 'Can anyone tell me what actually happened?' He could see his counterparts still working on the kid on the other trolley, the flat line on the monitor almost mocking them.

'Some kind of explosion. Lots of penetrating injuries. It

was outside a local factory. The kids were playing, waiting for their parents to finish their shifts.'

'Major Anderson,' a voice boomed through the resus room doors. Everyone froze for a second then immediately resumed what they'd been doing. Eyes glanced at each other and the noise level in the room plummeted.

Avery frowned at the uniformed figure in the doorway. He had three people standing nervously behind him. The rank was instantly recognisable—as was the glint of the two silver stars—and he could hardly hide his surprise. He'd never seen a major general in an ER before.

He looked to be in his fifties and had a mid-Western accent. He was well over six feet tall with broad shoulders and what looked like thick dark hair under his hat. There was something about him. An aura. An air. And it wasn't all about the rank. What had brought him to the ER? He could understand any major general in charge of a base this size wanting to be informed about incidents. He just wouldn't have expected him to attend personally.

Blake glanced upwards but didn't stop what he was doing. 'General Williams.'

The Major General was watching Blake carefully as he continued his resus attempts. 'I heard there was an explosion. Does your team require assistance?'

Blake kept working steadily. He glanced in Avery's direction but the Major General didn't follow his glance. He was focused on Blake.

'I have all the assistance I need. If anything changes, I'll let you know.'

'I'll expect an update in a few hours.'

'General.' Blake gave a nod in acknowledgement. He was attaching defibrillator pads to the young boy's chest. 'All clear.'

There was a short ping.

Avery was holding his breath and bent to pick up an

oxygen mask that had landed on the floor. Major General Williams turned to leave, his eyes lingering for a second on Avery.

Was he looking at him?

Two seconds later the major general disappeared down the corridor.

Avery straightened up, his gaze shifting around the people in the room. The noise level increased instantly. Katsuko was still bagging but her gaze was fixed on the door.

That was who he'd been looking at. What was going on there?

The male nurse he'd met earlier shouted towards the door, 'Two emergency theatres are open. The guy from the helipad is in the first one. We can take our kid to the other.'

There was a tiny second of silence, then it was broken with a little beep. Every head in the room turned. The monitor for the other patient. They finally had an output.

Avery paused as the doctor he hadn't even had a chance to meet yet raised his head from the bed. The look of pure relief on his face made him catch his breath. 'Do you need the theatre?' Avery asked.

He had to. This was another doctor's ER. He might be treating a patient but this was the military. He had to follow the chain of command.

Blake shook his head. 'No. I'm heading to paediatric ICU.' He frowned for a second. 'Do you need assistance?'

Avery shook his head. 'Is there a surgeon?'

Blake nodded.

'Then I'm good.' He turned back to the team. 'Right, get the IV fast-flowing, monitor his blood pressure.' He turned back at the nurse who'd threatened to break his hand. 'Are you good to bag?' He could see the determined tic in her jaw. There was no way she was leaving this patient.

Another nurse appeared at the door. 'We've another four

trauma cases—two paediatric, two adult and about twelve walking wounded.'

Avery glanced down at his now blood-splattered shirt. At some point he should really change. The radiographer walked back in and stuck the X-ray straight up on the light box, flicking the switch.

It didn't take a genius to see what was wrong. Both of Mahito's lungs were deflated. Oxygen wasn't circulating properly because of the penetrating chest injury. If there was no other choice, he could try to insert chest drains but it was unlikely the lungs could reinflate with the spear still in place. It would be foolish to attempt anything like that now—particularly when he had a theatre and surgeon at his disposal. Avery shook his head. 'Let's go, folks. We're never going to get these lungs to reinflate until we get this spear out of his chest. Someone point me in the direction of the theatre.'

'Let's go, people!' shouted Katsuko. For someone small and perfectly formed her voice had a real air of command. Everyone moved. Monitors were detached from the wall, oxygen canisters pushed under the trolley, a space blanket placed over the patient. Avery kept his eyes on the patient but after a second he looked up. They were all watching him expectantly.

There was something so reassuring about this. And he'd experienced it time and time again in the military. These people didn't know him. He'd walked into an emergency situation with only a wave of his ID. That was all he'd needed.

From that point on—early or not—he'd been expected to do his job. At first he'd been a bit concerned about the chaos. Now he realised everyone had known what to do, but the rush of blood and age of the child had fazed them all.

'Everyone ready?'

Eight heads nodded at him. 'Then, let's go.'

Hands remained pressed to a variety of areas on the little body. The move along the corridor was rapid. The theatre was on the same floor. The porter at the front of the procession swiped his card and held the doors open. A surgeon strode over and nodded at Avery, not even blinking that they didn't know each other.

Avery handed over the X-ray. 'Explosion at a local factory. This is Mahito. I don't have an age. Penetrating wound to the chest, two collapsed lungs, intubated but sats are poor.' He nodded at the monitor. 'Two IV lines, tachycardic at one-sixty and hypotensive. BP seventy over forty-five.'

He frowned. 'Sorry, didn't have time to catheterise.'

The surgeon shook his head. 'My staff will get to that. We'll take it from here.'

Theatre staff dressed in scrubs surrounded them, one set of hands replacing the others and a stern-looking woman taking over bagging duties from Katsuko. She moved away swiftly. It was the first time he'd actually seen her relinquish control to someone else.

The trolley moved forward, being pushed through another set of swing doors as the surgeon shouted orders.

Just like that.

Mahito was someone else's responsibility.

Avery looked down at his hands, smeared with blood. The rest of the staff turned and headed back out of the doors.

Katsuko folded her arms and glared at his hands.

'If you ever come into my ER again and touch a patient without washing your hands and putting on gloves, I will make sure you live to regret it.'

Her accent was odd. It had a lilt. A twang. Part Japanese, part American. Her English was completely and utterly fluent.

'And as for this…' She lifted her hand and picked his

fedora off his head. He'd completely forgotten about it. 'Who do you think you are, Indiana Jones?'

He let out a laugh. 'It's a pleasure to meet you too. And who said this was your ER?' He glanced over his shoulder. 'I was planning on making it mine.'

A spark flashed across her eyes. It was almost as if he'd issued a challenge.

There was a potent silence for a few seconds. Things had been chaotic before. Mahito had been the priority. Now the only noise around them was that of the swinging doors.

She was looking at him. Sizing him up. Did he meet the grade? His curiosity was sparked. What was the grade for the firecracker?

He couldn't help but start to smile. The air around them had a distinct sense of sizzle.

Despite the chaos of earlier her poker-straight hair had fallen back into place, framing her face perfectly. Those brown eyes could get him into a whole load of trouble. They hadn't even had a proper introduction yet, but Katsuko was one of the most gorgeous women he'd ever set eyes on. She might be small but she had curves in all the right places. One thing was for sure—if she was only six inches taller she would be on the catwalk.

It was odd. Avery had always gone for blondes—usually leggy. But all of a sudden leggy blondes had flown straight out of his mind.

She crossed her arms over her chest and met his inquisitive gaze. From the determined tilt of her chin it was clear she knew he'd been checking her out.

She plonked his hat back on his head, then turned and walked away, giving him a clear view of her tight, perfectly formed ass. The pale green scrubs looked good on her.

He couldn't help but laugh.

Shaking his head, he walked after her, stopping at the nearest sink to wash his hands. He didn't even have time to catch his breath. The siren sounded again and another trolley crashed through the doors from an ambulance outside. This time the patient was an adult. His colour was poor and he was rasping.

The ambulance crew spoke rapidly in Japanese. Katsuko didn't even blink, she just translated. 'Thirty-five-year-old also injured in the factory explosion. Bruising across his torso already visible. No penetration wounds. They suspect broken ribs. Poor oxygen saturation. He's complained of chest pain and he's tachycardic. Probably tension pneumothorax.' She bit her lip. 'First the kid, now the adult.'

She was mirroring his exact thoughts. Two cases of pneuomothorax, each requiring different management.

In their absence, someone had cleared the resus room. Both bays were empty again. Avery grabbed the pink stethoscope that was hanging around Katsuko's neck.

'Hey!' she shouted.

'Needs must. Haven't been able to find mine yet.'

As the trolley eased to a halt he listened carefully to both sides of the man's chest. He waved his hand. 'Sit him forward so I can check his back.' Two nursing assistants responded instantly, helping to sit the man forward. The back was clear. No sign of any wounds. The patient was eased back. The shift in the trachea was evident. There was no need for anything else. A pneumothorax was air in the chest cavity. This had probably resulted from a fractured rib puncturing his lung and releasing air into the pleural space. A pneumothorax wasn't usually life-threatening unless it progressed to a tension pneumothorax, causing compression of the vena cava, reducing cardiac blood flow to the heart and decreasing cardiac output—and that was exactly what had happened here.

A tension pneumothorax could be life-threatening and needed prompt action. The military had collected vast amounts of data regarding tension pneumothorax and subsequent treatment. In a combat setting, tension pneumothorax was the second leading cause of death, and was often preventable. Today Avery was going to make sure it was preventable.

'Tension pneumothorax.'

Two words were all it took. Packs opened around him. Surgical gloves appeared. He pulled them on and swabbed the skin. Katsuko was speaking into the man's ear in a low voice. She waved Avery on with a nod of her head.

'Let's get some oxygen on the patient.'

The staff responded instantly.

'Do we have a name?'

His body was already starved of oxygen. They had to supplement as much as possible.

One of the physician's assistants put his hand in the man's pocket and pulled out a wallet. 'Akio Yamada.' He frowned as he calculated in his head. 'I make him forty-four.'

Avery leaned over the man. His eyes were tightly closed and he was wincing, obviously in pain. He put his hand gently on his shoulder. 'Akio, I'm a doctor. I'm going to do something that will help your breathing. It might be a little uncomfortable.'

This wasn't a pleasant procedure but the effect would be almost instant relief. Air was trapped and had caused the man's lung to collapse. As soon as the pressure was relieved and the lung reinflated he'd be able to breathe more easily again. Katsuko gave a nod that she'd finished translating.

There were specially manufactured needles designed just for a tension pneumothorax. Avery held out his hand. 'Fourteen-gauge needle and catheter.' He'd done this on numerous occasions in the past. It only took a few seconds to feel with his fingers for the second intercostal space, at the midclavicular line. It was vital that the needle be inserted at a ninety-degree angle to the chest wall so it would be positioned directly into the pleural space. Any mistake could result in a chance of hitting other structures—even the heart. But Avery was experienced.

The room was silent during the procedure. In a few seconds there was an audible release as the trapped air rushed out and the tension was released from his chest. Avery removed the needle and disposed of it, leaving the catheter in place. He secured it with some tape as he watched the man's chest. Sometimes the lung inflated again immediately, sometimes it took a little time. The patient would need to be monitored.

He pulled off his gloves. 'Can we keep an eye on his sats for the next few hours and get a portable chest X-ray?' The man's eyes flickered open.

Avery put a hand on his shoulder. It didn't matter that the patient couldn't understand him. 'You should feel easier now. Just relax. We'll keep a close eye on you.'

Katsuko's gaze met his and she translated again. At least, he hoped she was translating. The truth was she could be saying anything at all and he'd never know. In a way it frustrated him. When he'd thought he was being shipped out to Portugal and Italy he'd learned a few words and phrases that he could use in clinical situations to reassure patients. He'd need to try and learn some basic Japanese.

'Doctor?'

A clerk was standing at the door. 'Yes?'

She waved an electronic tablet at him. 'I'll need you to write some notes on the two patients you've seen and fill some orders.' She hesitated for a second. 'Because you're not officially on duty yet I'll need to get another doctor to sign off on your cases.'

He met her worried gaze with a smile. 'No problem.' He could almost hear her inaudible sigh. Was she really worried he'd be offended? Of course he wasn't.

He turned back to the patient. The male African-

American nurse he'd met earlier had appeared back in the room. This time he held out his large hand towards Avery. 'Frank Kelly, pleased to meet you.' Avery had thought he was big at six feet two, but this guy was a giant. With his regular runs and gym workouts he normally felt pretty fit, but Frank would make a professional wrestler shrink away.

'I'll take over, Katsuko,' Frank said confidently. 'The other two majors are fractures, one a femur, the other a humerus and shoulder displacement. Do you want to check them over? Katia is triaging the walking wounded.'

Katsuko paused. He could see her hesitation to hand another patient over. Didn't she let anyone else take charge?

He tried to hide his smile and he turned back to the patient. The colour in his cheeks was gradually improving.

He scribbled some instructions on a chart for Frank. 'I'll write him up for some pain relief and order a chest X-ray. Can you monitor his obs every ten minutes for the next hour?'

Frank nodded. The smile seemed to remain permanently on his face. Avery's gaze followed Katsuko as she washed her hands and left the room. He turned back to Frank, whose knowing smile had got even wider.

'Watch out, new boy, she bites.'

The professional thing to do was to pretend he had no idea what Frank was talking about but somehow he knew that wouldn't wash. Besides, he was curious.

'What's that supposed to mean?'

Frank shrugged and pushed the button on the machine to inflate the blood-pressure cuff. He was laughing away to himself.

'Frank?'

Frank shook his head. 'Just remember who her father is.'

Now he was really curious. 'Why? Who is her father?'

Frank raised his eyebrows. 'That would be Donald Williams.' He paused for a second. '*Major General* Donald Williams. Our commander.'

Avery couldn't help his head flicking sideways. It didn't matter that Katsuko's retreating back was nowhere in sight.

Of course. That was why the Major General had been looking at her. A giant of a man, notoriously strict, he'd commanded this base for over ten years. He also had pale skin.

There was no family resemblance at all.

'Donald Williams is Katsuko's father?'

Frank nodded. 'Sure is.' His eyes gleamed. 'And watch out because he bites too, especially anyone who looks at his daughter the way you do.'

CHAPTER TWO

A TEN-HOUR SHIFT had turned into a fourteen-hour shift. There was no way she was going back home when the ER waiting room was so full that patients couldn't find seats.

After a few hours some of the local police arrived to collect statements and details of injuries. 'Any idea what happened?'

The first one nodded. 'Delivery mistake. Chemicals for the printing factory had been mislabelled. They got mixed together as they normally do and...*boom*.'

Katsuko sucked in a breath. It all seemed so matter-of-fact. She'd seen exactly the damage those mislabelled chemicals had caused. The man who had been brought in by helicopter had died. Mahito was currently in their paediatric ICU. It would be a few days before they'd even attempt to wake him up from his induced coma.

Her paperwork was finally finished. The next shift had come on duty and all patients were currently being seen.

There was a nudge at her shoulder. 'How about you show the new guy where he can get some food?'

Avery. That was his name. These US doctors rolled in, dated their way around every department and rolled back out without a second glance. Did he really think he was the first new doctor to show a spark of interest in her?

He leaned against the wall next to her, folding his arms, his Indiana Jones style hat back on his head.

'I can't believe you actually walk about like that.'

He tipped his hat at her. 'What can I say? It's a precious family heirloom. I don't leave home without it.'

At some point he'd changed into a set of obligatory pale green scrubs. They suited him, matched his pale green eyes. There was a borrowed stethoscope around his neck and his military boots were still in place. His feet must be aching.

His blond hair was longer than normal for the military—most of the men had buzz cuts around here. She resisted the temptation to smile. Her father would have a fit. As soon as that tiny bit of forward-flopping hair touched his eyebrow there would be memos flying about the base.

He was still smiling at her. A lazy, sexy grin. This guy was movie-star material and he knew it. That rankled.

Now that he was dressed in thin scrubs she could see practically every outlined and defined muscle on his chest and arms. The scrubs were cutting into the muscle around the top of his arm. It was clear he worked out.

Another one. Cheeky. Sassy. Following her about the place. Most scattered when they found out who her father was. Well, not really her father, but as good as. The odd newcomer had thought it a challenge to try and date the Major General's daughter. But she'd learned quickly.

It had only taken overhearing one conversation. A few sentences from one airman to another—that dating the General's daughter would be a fast track to promotion—to make her stomach turn over and her blood boil.

She was immune. Immune to the too-long hair, twinkling eyes and defined muscles. She was immune to the cheeky innuendo and admiring glances.

No matter how cute the overall package.

'I'm sure you can find someone else to show you where to eat.'

'But what if I want you to show me?'

She shot him a beaming smile. 'I'm busy.'

He lifted her stethoscope off her neck. 'No. You're not. Your duty shift finished four hours ago.'

She raised her eyebrows. 'And yours doesn't even start until tomorrow.'

He placed his hand across his heart. 'Just shows you what kind of guy I am. Dedicated. Hard-working. Selfless.'

She grabbed her stethoscope back and started to walk down the corridor towards the changing rooms. 'Big-headed.'

'Ouch.' He gave a little stagger against a wall. He was still smiling at her. 'First Lieutenant Williams, is that how you treat a fellow airman?' He'd raised his voice a little and she could see heads turning in their direction. He opened his arms. 'I've travelled halfway around the world. Billeted here at short notice. Walked in and worked a fourteen-hour shift.' He shrugged his shoulders at two other amused staff members walking towards them. 'I didn't have time to check in with the housing officer and find out where I'm staying, let alone have something to eat.' He gave them a conspiratorial smile. 'Is this the kind of welcome Okatu gives new staff members?'

Katsuko felt the rush of heat into her cheeks. This guy was actually getting to her a little.

Caleb, one of the nurses, shook his head as he moved past and tutted. 'Shocking.' It was obvious he was trying not to laugh.

'Not so much as a cup of coffee,' added Seiko, one of the aerospace medical technicians.

It was odd. Avery's grin was almost infectious. She could feel the edges of her mouth turning upwards even though she was willing them not to. She might not have paid enough attention before, but he did look tired. Who knew how many hours he'd travelled before he'd done an unexpected shift? And she couldn't remember him taking a break at any point. The guy must be starving.

Avery shrugged. 'Or maybe you have someone waiting for you at home?'

The flush in her cheeks warmed even more. Nothing like asking if she was single. What was worse was that she could see the exchange of glances between her colleagues.

Katsuko threw up her hands. 'Fine. Fine.' She glanced at her watch. 'I'll phone Barney, the housing officer, and we can pick up your keys before I show you where to eat.'

'Food!' exclaimed Avery. 'It's been so long I don't even remember what it tastes like.'

He was walking right alongside her, so close their arms were almost brushing together. She bumped him with her hip and laughed as he lost his balance. 'Cut it out, drama king. I'll give you ten minutes to shower and get back into your dress uniform. If you're not outside in ten I'm leaving you behind.'

He gave her a wink as he backed into the changing room. 'Not a chance. I'm all yours.'

She gulped. The new guy was too smart for his own good. Too sassy. And a whole lot too sexy.

One of her colleagues gave her a nudge. 'Hmm… Dr Flynn? Is he single? Because if he is, I'll fight you for him.'

Ten minutes later she emerged from the changing room and walked straight into the chest of Avery Flynn.

'Oof!'

He grinned. 'I got you back. And at least I didn't leave you sprawling on the floor.'

She straightened her blue jacket. She'd spent longer than she usually did getting changed. For some strange reason she'd felt the urge to check her make-up and spray on some perfume.

'Maybe next time you won't get in the way.'

If he'd looked good in the scrubs he looked even better in the dress uniform. The pale blue shirt and dark jacket fitted his frame perfectly. His eyes swept up and down her quickly, taking in the regulation skirt, her legs no longer hidden in scrubs. She resisted the temptation to clear her throat.

He waved his arm in front of him. 'Lead on, then, First Lieutenant. I'd hate to get in the way.'

She rolled her eyes and started walking. 'Are you always going to be this annoying?'

His backpack was slung over his shoulder and his darned fedora was in his other hand. At least he wasn't trying to wear it while he was in uniform. He fell into step alongside her. 'Believe me, I've got annoying down to a fine art.'

He pushed open the door and held it for her. She swept through in front of him. 'I bet you have.'

She pointed in one direction. 'Let's go this way. We'll pick up your keys from the housing officer. I gave him a call and he told me where he'd leave things for you.'

Avery frowned and looked at his watch. 'Is that the time? I'd no idea it was so late.' He nudged her with his elbow. 'Just as well I'm with you. The housing office would be closed at ten o'clock at night.'

She started crossing the road. 'It might surprise you but we have lots of night-time deployment flights. The housing officer has a page. He wouldn't have minded if you'd called him out.'

He gave her a curious glance. 'Lived here long?'

'Almost all my life.'

His footsteps faltered a little but she didn't halt. She knew exactly what would happen next. He lengthened his stride and walked a little in front of her, turning around to catch sight of her face. 'I didn't think that was possible.'

'It's not.'

He wasn't going to be put off with her short answers.

By this point, he was almost walking backwards, keeping his gaze on her the whole time.

'So how have you managed it?'

He was so busy watching her face that he wasn't paying attention to the road. She reached out and grabbed him just as his foot hit a small rut.

His reaction was automatic. As his balance tipped he grabbed her hand that was clutching the front of his jacket. The warm skin of the palm of his hand wrapped firmly around her wrist. It was like slow motion. A flood of electricity shot up her arm towards her chest. If she could have snatched her hand back she would have.

But he hadn't let go. His pale green eyes fixed on hers. Nothing was said. Neither of them moved again. Her breath caught some way in her throat and all of a sudden she felt the desperate urge to find something to drink. Preferably alcohol.

'Can't have you falling for me twice in one day.'

It was meant to come out as a quip—a joke. But the intensity of his gaze made her normally firm voice turn into a whisper.

He responded instantly. 'Oh, I think we can.' There was an edge to his voice, a raspiness she hadn't noticed before, that sent a shiver straight down her spine.

Her fingers slowly let go of his jacket. Avery stared at his hand for a few seconds before finally letting go of her wrist.

There was a tiny shake of his head, as if he was trying to process what had just happened.

'Over here.' She spoke quickly, pointing to an office block. 'That's where we'll get your keys.' She strode ahead. It was crazy. But this guy was unsettling her. Touching her. Giving her glimpses of a whole other world out there.

She buzzed them into the block and picked up his keys and a map of the base from the reception desk. She glanced at the key fob and circled a place on the map with a pen.

'Look, we're here. And we'll probably go and eat in this street here. Your house is over here. It's about ten minutes from where we'll eat.'

She was conscious of him leaning over the map beside her. Even though they'd been close up earlier in the ER she hadn't noticed the woody smell of his aftershave. Maybe he'd just put some on? Just like she had...

And that darned bit of hair at the front fell over his forehead. Her fingers itched to push it back.

He picked up the map and turned towards her, their noses almost touching. As it was night-time the reception area wasn't brightly lit. There was no one else around. It was almost...intimate.

She stepped back and sucked in a breath. His head tilted to the side a little, as if he was surprised by her sudden movement. What was he used to? Women falling at his feet?

'There's a courtyard five minutes away.' She moved over towards the door again. 'What is that you want to eat?'

As if on cue his stomach gave a loud growl and he put his hand over his belly and laughed. 'Something that no doctor would approve of.'

She pushed open the door. 'Like what? You've just arrived in Japan. Don't you want to try some local cuisine?'

He shook his head. 'Not tonight. Tonight I'm ravenous. If I'm sampling genuine Japanese food I want to savour every mouthful. Think of me as a horse.'

She turned to face him. 'Are you crazy?'

'Yes, I am. It's called low blood sugar. I just want to stick my head in a bucket and eat and eat until I'm ready to collapse in a corner. I want calorie-laden carbs. Can you find me some?'

She wagged her finger at him. 'Sure I can. But I'm warning you, this is blackmail material.'

His eyes twinkled. 'Well, I can't think of anyone I'd rather have blackmail me.'

* * *

Five minutes later they reached a pizza place and slid into a booth. The smell was enough to make him keel over. Food. He needed food.

He clocked a buffet in the corner. 'Let's not wait. How about we just go to the buffet?'

He could see the ready-cooked pizzas under the heat lamps. They were practically calling out his name. His hand was poised on the table, ready to get back up again.

Katsuko laughed and shook her head. 'What do you want to drink?'

He looked around. 'A beer. I'll have a beer. I'll probably sleep for a week.'

She gestured to one of the waitresses. 'Just make sure you're ready for your shift tomorrow. If you don't appear on time, remember—' she pointed to the key that was still in his hand '—I know where you live.'

He couldn't help the instant grin that appeared. He paused for a second and stared at the key dangling from his hand. 'Yeah, you do, don't you?'

He hadn't quite meant to say it like that. But it had just naturally come out that way. He locked gazes with those dark brown eyes. He wanted to get closer. He wanted to see if they were flecked with gold, or if the dark brown was as intense as it looked from here.

She licked her lips and his feet instantly shifted. The waitress appeared next to them, talking rapidly in Japanese. Avery pulled down his jacket and moved over to the buffet. He couldn't help but shake his head. He hadn't slept and had barely eaten in nearly two days. He was flirting with a colleague. No, he was getting fresh with the base commander's daughter. He was clearly losing his mind.

He picked up a heated plate and put two slices on it.

Katsuko appeared at his side. 'Did you even look?' She was smiling and had a glass of wine in her hand.

She picked up a plate and put two slices of pizza and some salad on it. 'Remember your five a day,' she whispered, then added a spoonful of salad to his plate.

Avery stared down at his plate. 'Sorry,' he murmured. 'At last count it was around forty-eight hours since I had some proper food.'

She gave a knowing nod. 'Is it the joys of being an ER doctor, or the joys of being in the air force?'

They returned to the booth and he spent the next few minutes eating. It appeared he'd picked two slices of pepperoni and mushroom pizza and they hit all the right spots. After a few minutes he rested back in the booth and picked up his bottle of beer.

The cold liquid felt like nectar sliding down his throat.

Katsuko was sipping her wine and eating her pizza with a knife and fork. She raised her eyebrows at him. 'Finally feeling human again?'

He nodded. The horrible churning feeling in his stomach had abated. After the long travel, the working hours and the fast eating, he should be ready to lie down and go straight to sleep.

But there was no way he wanted to sleep when he had the sparkiest woman he'd ever met in front of him.

'You know, we haven't even been properly introduced.'

She frowned for a second. 'Yes, we have.'

He shook his head. 'Oh, no, we haven't. You threatened to break my hand.'

The expression on her face softened a little. 'Yes, I did.' It was as if she were reliving the memory.

He held out his hand towards her. 'Captain Avery Flynn, doctor. I'm from Ohio but have been stationed in just about every air force base that's ever existed. Joined as soon as I qualified. Been in the service now for eight years.'

He held his breath. She waited a few seconds, then wiped her hands on her napkin and reached out her hand for his.

There it was again. That tiny little buzz. He hadn't been imagining it.

Her hand was cooler than his. But it seemed to fit in his grasp.

'First Lieutenant Katsuko Williams. I joined when I was eighteen and did my nurse training. I did a few months in Georgia to complete my nurse training. The rest of the time I've been based here.'

She gently withdrew her hand from his and took another sip of her wine.

He looked at her carefully. In the brighter lights of the pizza place he could see just how flawless her skin was and just how dark her eyes were. No gold flecks. No trace of another colour. Just pure, deep, dark brown.

'Katsuko's a nice name. What does it mean?'

'You think my name means something?'

He shrugged. 'Everyone's name means something. Mine is French—it means wise.'

She let out a laugh and he raised his eyebrows. 'Or, if you're a fan of *Lord of the Rings*, it means ruling with elf wisdom in English.'

She spluttered. 'You're joking!'

He shook his head. 'I'm not.' He waved his phone at her. 'Want to check it?'

'No.' She waved over the waitress and spoke quickly. The waitress gave him a knowing smile and walked away.

'What did you say to her?'

'I ordered more drinks.'

'Trying to get me drunk?'

'As if.' She leaned across the table towards him.

He hesitated. What was she doing? Was she actually flirting with him? No one could deny the electricity in the air around them or the occasional little gleam in her eye. But Katsuko Williams didn't strike him as a woman to mess with. And that just made him like her all the more. So he couldn't resist. He leaned forward too.

She looked him straight in the eye. 'Victorious child.'

'What?' He was confused. So *not* what he'd thought she might say.

She sat back, looking pleased with herself. 'You asked me what my name meant.'

He blinked. She pulled her shirt a little straighter over the curves of her breasts. From the expression on her face it was clear she knew *exactly* what she was doing. She was playing him.

He pushed his plate away and pressed his forehead on the table with a sigh.

'What are you doing?'

He turned his head to the side. 'I'm done. I've travelled too far. I've eaten too much. Worked for too long. And now my local tour guide is being mean to me.'

She gave a snort. 'Mean to you?'

He looked up through the floppy part of his hair—he really needed to get that cut. 'Yes, mean to me.'

She folded her arms across her chest and he sat back up.

He liked her. She was smart. And direct. Maybe even a little bit quirky. This flirting could lead somewhere. He didn't do long-term. But he could be here for up to six months. She could make those six months fun. 'Victorious child. I like it. But it doesn't quite have an elf-like ring to it. What was the other name they called you?'

She rolled her eyes and picked up her wine glass again. 'Nothing.'

She didn't like her nickname? Interesting. 'It wasn't nothing. It was *faya*-something.'

She sipped at her wine. 'Only close friends get to call me that.'

He was curious. Could he get to be in that category?

'Say it for me again?'

She sighed. *'Faiyakuraka.'*

He scrunched up his face and tried to concentrate on the sounds. *'Fay-acure-aka.'* He leaned back, feeling pleased with himself. 'Firecracker.'

'Not even close. You need to work on your accent.'

He took a drink from his beer bottle. 'Will you help me with that?'

This time Katsuko dropped her head on the table. 'Give me strength. Do you ever stop?'

'Not if I don't have to.'

He pushed her head back up. 'Hey, it's my first time in Japan. I'm learning. Why shouldn't I learn with a beautiful colleague?'

Something flashed across her face and he instantly knew it had been the wrong thing to say. Great. He tried to cover his tracks quickly.

'Talking of accents, I thought you said you'd stayed here most of your life. Your accent is distinctly American.'

She gave a little nod. 'And when I speak Japanese, my accent is distinctly Japanese.'

He was confused. 'What do you mean?'

Her eyes fixed on the corner of the room. 'Let's just say I'm kind of caught between two worlds.'

It was a strange thing to say. And it wasn't just the words. It was the delivery of them. As if she wasn't entirely happy.

It felt too personal to pry. He barely knew her. He was brand new around here and he didn't want to do anything that would upset a colleague.

He gave a smile. 'So, what's it like being the daughter of the commander?'

The unsettled feeling on her face vanished. She gave a little shake of her head. 'Oh, you have no idea.' She lifted her wine glass again and took a careful sip. 'Let's just say that the man you saw today is not the man that I live with.'

Avery set his beer bottle down. This conversation was

getting more curious by the minute. The man he'd seen today had been like most other major generals he'd met in his career—someone not to be messed with.

Katsuko was biting her bottom lip as her fingers ran up the stem of her wine glass. It was as if she were contemplating what to say.

'So he's a different man behind closed doors? I just can't imagine that.' Avery leaned back against the booth.

She met his gaze. 'He's not really my father.'

'He's not?' He couldn't help it. The words just came out. 'But Frank said…' His voice tailed off.

'I know. Everyone says that. Because that's what everyone really knows. Don was a pilot—my dad was his RIO. They had to eject from a plane during a combat mission and my father hit his head on the cockpit. He died instantly.'

Avery felt his mouth instantly dry. 'Wow. I'm sorry.'

She held up her hands. 'Didn't you spot the family resemblance?' When he didn't answer she shrugged. 'My dad was African-American, my mother Japanese.'

'What happened to your mom?'

'She became unwell just after my dad died. Everyone thought she was grieving—maybe they even thought she was depressed. It turned out she had leukaemia.'

Avery shook his head. This story was getting worse and worse.

Katsuko flicked open her wallet. 'Here they are.' She turned her wallet around. Behind the plastic inset was an old photo. Even though it was behind the plastic it was a little weathered around the edges—as if it was pulled out frequently—and the colours were a little faded.

He leaned forward to get a better view. It was a close-up of a couple laughing together. The woman had her arms wrapped around the man's neck. She was a petite, beautiful Japanese woman with long straight dark hair wearing a bright red top. The African-American man was much taller and dressed in his uniform. He was laughing too, staring straight at his wife. It was obvious they were in love. Even though the photo was old it was like a little moment captured in time. The love emanated from it.

He looked up. Katsuko was staring at the photo, lost in the memory. It was like a fist grasping inside his chest and squeezing his heart. He'd never experienced anything so intense. Her finger traced over the photo and she gave a sad smile. 'They look really happy together,' he said.

She looked up. 'They were. My dad said that he had to court my mom. She pretended to be very traditional to begin with, even though she was secretly more like a rebel. He even learned some Japanese to try and win her round.'

'What did he learn?' He'd struggled to get his tongue around even a few words today. He'd have to learn the basics for working in the ER. No matter where he worked, he always tried to learn a few words of the language. Japanese just seemed a little trickier than most. Maybe Katsuko could help him?

She shook her head and met his gaze. 'Oh, I don't want to give away any of my dad's secrets. Before I know it you'll be using them on all the women in the base.'

'Maybe not all the women.' The words came out naturally. He couldn't help but flirt with her. He'd be crazy not to.

She laughed at him. 'You think you're good at this, don't you?'

He laughed back. 'Only when I'm jet-lagged or drunk.' He stared at his bottle. 'I'm not sure which one I am right now.'

She gave a nod and glanced back at the photo, touching it with her index finger. *'Kokoro no sokokara aishiteru.'* It was almost a whisper.

He bent forward. 'What did you say?'

She shook her head. '*Kokoro no sokokara aishiteru.* It's just something my dad used to say to me as a little girl.'

Now he was really curious. 'What does it mean?'

She made a face. 'I guess the literal translation would be, "I love you from the bottom of my heart." But when my father used to say it he pressed his hand to my face and then to his chest. It was more like, "You have my heart."'

'That's lovely.' It wasn't really an expression he used much. Most guys in the world didn't describe things as lovely. But it seemed right. 'You must miss them so much.'

She closed her wallet and pressed her lips together. 'I do—just like any kid would. In a way, I was lucky, even though it didn't feel like that. I didn't lose them both together. That would have been worse. My mother helped me through the death of my father, and she helped prepare me for her own death. She, and Don.'

'So, the General adopted you?'

'He had to. It was the only way I could stay on the base. He wasn't a major general then. And he'd never married.' She toyed with her glass. 'Apparently long before anything happened to my parents they'd named him as my guardian in their will. I guess they just never really expected him to have to act as it.'

'Didn't your mother have other family?'

Katsuko shifted in her seat. 'My grandmother lives in Tokyo. She wasn't well enough to cope with a ten-year-old. She has rheumatoid arthritis. She's in a wheelchair now. I visit—I've always visited—but she hates Don with a passion. And she didn't like the fact that my mother had married an American. It seems I can't really do anything to please her.' There was a wistful tone to her voice.

The edges of her lips turned upwards in a forced smile. 'Don's great. He's always treated me as if I was his own. He tells me I'm the daughter he never had. But sometimes I feel like him adopting me might have ruined his chances of ever meeting anyone else. He and Dad were best friends. I was so used to being around him that when both my parents died I never even thought I could end up anywhere else.' She licked her lips and stared at the table for a second. 'I remember when my mother was really ill he came and sat with her. My mother held my hand and told me that when she went to sleep I'd go and stay with Don.'

Avery reached over and squeezed her hand. He'd been in the air force for years. He'd worked on servicemen who had been injured in action and sometimes even killed. He'd dealt with sick family members. But he'd never met a kid who'd been orphaned. He couldn't even imagine what that felt like.

Katsuko's gaze fixed on their joined hands for a few moments. Then she pulled her hand back against her chest.

Avery licked his lips. 'Frank says the Major General bites.'

There was a millisecond of confusion on her face before the comment obviously fell into context.

'Frank should learn to mind his own business.'

Avery drummed his fingers on the table. 'Just as a matter of curiosity, how often has he bitten?'

The words hung in the air between them. It was ridiculous and he knew that. He'd only just met her.

He'd been stationed on air force bases before. There were always people you clicked with straight away—hospitals were like that. But he had always been a little cautious. He liked to get know a woman before he decided if wanted to date them. And he didn't do long-term—not with the kind of family he had. His relationships only lasted as long as his posting at the base.

He didn't generally do things on impulse. Not like this.

He might as well have painted on the table between them, *I like you.*

It made him feel a little odd. He had no idea what was normal for Katusko. Maybe she did date servicemen that she knew weren't there permanently? Maybe that suited her as much as it suited him. But somehow the curl in his stomach was telling him not to count on it.

'I can look after myself,' she said sharply as she waved to the waitress. 'Can we have the check, please?'

The waitress nodded and pulled the prepared check from her uniform.

Avery reached over and grabbed it. On the air base you could pay in dollars or yen. Luckily he had both. It was the one thing he had been able to organise.

Katsuko pulled some notes from her pocket but he shook his head. 'Let me. You found me my keys, somewhere to eat and hopefully you'll point me in the direction of my house.'

He could tell she secretly wanted to argue but he handed the money straight to the waitress and slid out from the booth. 'Shall we?'

She picked up her jacket and followed him out into the balmy night air. She nodded her head to the side. 'This way.'

He swung his bag over his shoulder and fell into step alongside her. She pointed to places as they walked along. 'Down that street is the high school. At the bottom of that road is the swimming pool. And there's a golf course if you're interested.'

He was watching her carefully. She seemed so comfortable in her own skin. He liked that in a woman. She was confident at work and confident in her personal life. She'd only revealed a tiny part of herself to him tonight but he definitely wanted to find out more. He stopped walking and looked at her. 'Aren't we doing this the wrong way? Shouldn't I be walking you home?'

'That would only work if this was a date. And this definitely *isn't* a date.'

'It's not? Darn it.' He couldn't help but smile.

She stopped under a streetlight and turned towards him. She had a smile on her face too. 'Are you always this infuriating?'

He leaned forward a little, stopping just a few inches from her face.

It was ridiculous. He wanted to kiss her. He really wanted to kiss her. But she was difficult to read and the last thing he could afford to do was upset a work colleague by making an unwanted move.

She was staring right at him with those dark, dark eyes.

There was no one else around them. The street was completely empty. But he still whispered. 'Why don't you hang around and find out?'

Katsuko blinked. The smile stayed on her face and her eyebrows rose just a little.

She spun away, leaving her scent trailing around him, a mixture of jasmine and amber. He had to resist the temptation to inhale the scent completely.

She glanced over her shoulder as she kept walking. 'Come on, lazy boy. Your house is just around the corner.' She had an easiness about her, a casualness that he could easily misconstrue. His brain might be addled from the long journey, the travel, and not helped by the two beers but he was finding her pretty mesmerising.

She stopped in front of a standard air force house and pointed to the number on the door. He swung his pack from his shoulder and pulled out the key. 'Let me dump my bag and I'll walk you back to yours.'

He put his key in the lock and opened the front door. Her amber and jasmine scents were swept away by a musty odour. Katsuko let out a laugh. 'Uh-oh. Remind me to buy you some air freshener.'

He winced, reaching inside the front door to flick on the light. 'Do you think the whole place smells like this?'

She wrinkled her nose. 'All I know is, if you report for duty tomorrow smelling like that, no one will work with you. It's damp. Like a men's locker room.'

'And how do you know what a men's locker room smells like?'

She gave him a wink.

A wink. An actual wink.

'We all have our secrets.' She walked past him down the hall and opened a cupboard.

For around half a second earlier tonight he'd thought of backing off. Once she'd shared about her mum and dad and her painful past he'd wondered if Katsuko would really be the kind of girl who would be up for a fling.

But he'd kept flirting with her and she was flirting right back. Katsuko Williams was proving hard to resist, no matter how many red flags were flying in the back of his head.

'I'll let you find your own way around your new home. All I need to show you is this.' She held up a bag.

'What's that?'

'Earthquake emergency kit. Dry rations, drinking water, basic medical supplies. There's a hard hat and gloves too. Oh, and a flashlight.'

'Will I need it?' He didn't really like the sound of that.

She put the kit back down and held up her hands. 'You're in Japan now, Avery. This is earthquake central. We average a thousand a year and have more drills than you could ever know. Just be sure to keep your shoes and flashlight next to your bed. They'll send you on training in the next few days.' She stepped right up under his nose and tapped a finger on his chest. 'You'll soon be saying "Drop, cover, hold" in your sleep.'

She turned to walk away and waved her hand. 'Nice to meet you, Captain Flynn. Go on now, get to bed and try and get rid of those huge bags under your eyes. Don't worry about me. I can find my own way home.'

She'd already started to walk slowly back down the path and he felt an unexpected pang of disappointment.

'I can walk you. I will. Let me lock up.'

She stopped walking and turned around, illuminated by the streetlight behind her outlining her figure and framing her face perfectly. 'No. It's best you don't.'

Whoa. He sucked in a breath. *Was he watching a scene from a movie? That was what this looked like.*

His hand was already on the key but he stopped. She'd said no. The chivalrous part of him wanted to argue, but his rational head told him that Katsuko had lived here since she was a child. She knew this base like the back of her hand. She could find her way home safely without his help.

He paused in the doorway. 'Katsuko?'

She looked up.

'Thank you. Thank you for tonight.'

She gave a little nod.

He leaned against the doorjamb. It would be so easy to go on inside but he wanted to watch her walk away. Her outline was silhouetted as she strolled down the street. Her uniform hugged her curves well and there was a sass to her step. His head leaned against the doorpost. Fatigue was washing over him now. At the bottom of the street she turned again and shouted, 'Hey! Avery?'

His head shot back up. 'Yeah?'

'The answer to your earlier question—'

His earlier question?

'—is only when I tell him.' She was grinning broadly as she rounded the corner.

His brain tried to kick into gear. He closed the door behind him and tried not to inhale the smell. It would be windows open tonight. It didn't really matter anyway. He never stayed anywhere for too long.

A spark went off. And he smiled. The question. It had been about the Major General. *How often has he bitten?*

He couldn't wipe the smile off his face as he went to find the bedroom.

CHAPTER THREE

HE WAS ALREADY there when she arrived for duty the next morning.

And yep. She liked him just as much in his scrubs as she did in his dress uniform. Darn it.

'How did you get on last night?' Frank nudged her at the front desk.

'What do you mean?'

The old rogue's eyes were twinkling and she felt herself start to bristle. She had a horrible feeling she knew where this would go. Nothing on this base was a secret. 'I heard you took the new boy out for something to eat, then showed him back to his place. Get back late last night?' He nudged her again. Twice.

There was a giggle behind her. Seiko. The aerospace medical technician who had seen her with Avery outside the changing rooms.

'Don't be ridiculous. Nothing happened.' She glared at Seiko and turned back to Frank. 'And if I find out you're saying anything else...'

Frank held up his hands and laughed as he walked away. 'He's a good-looking guy. Got to get in there quick. Who knows who else might decide to get friendly with him?'

Something uncomfortable crept down her spine. She didn't even want to think about that. And that was even more ridiculous because she hadn't even thought to ask him last night about his family. Or any attachments. Or any children.

She felt sick. For a few seconds last night she'd thought he might actually kiss her. Even more ridiculous. You couldn't just meet a guy and let him kiss you. News like that would sweep around the base quicker than a new karaoke song. She'd no intention of being the subject of anyone's gossip. Her father would flip.

He'd intervened twice that she knew of. And even though she'd joked with Avery last night, she'd never asked him to intervene. One guy had been boasting about dating the General's daughter—and boasting about a bit more than that. He'd ended up at a different base in Japan. Another guy who'd told her he was single had been mysteriously transferred after a few months of heavy dating. She'd heard later through the grapevine that he'd had a pregnant fiancée back in the US who was also in the service.

Neither guy had ever been mentioned but the General didn't take kindly to anyone making a fool of her.

Trouble was, Avery was kind of fun. And fun was what she needed right now. She might even have to warn the General off.

She'd heard Blake mention earlier that they weren't even sure how long his posting would be as he was covering for someone else. Her brain was telling her to back off. But she couldn't get over how comfortable she'd been around him—or how one look had given her a tiny buzz she'd never experienced before.

Even if it was only for a few weeks or months, what was the harm in seeing Avery Flynn?

She stalked down the corridor and checked the board to see how many patients were in the ER. A little voice drifted down the corridor towards her. 'You smell funny.'

'Do I?'

She almost laughed out loud. She peeked around into the cubicle. Avery was talking to a little girl with blonde curly hair. She was sitting on her father's knee as Avery bent in front of her. The father, First Lieutenant Bruce, caught Katsuko's eye and cringed.

'Hi, Abigail. What is it today?'

She walked behind the curtain and knelt down next to Avery. The tidal wave of fresh aftershave swept over her. She tried to keep her face straight as she mumbled under her breath. 'Wow. You've overdone that a bit.'

His eyes darted towards her and she thought he might actually blush, but he kept his cool and his brow furrowed. 'You've met Abigail before?'

Katsuko nodded solemnly. 'Abigail seems to like us here.' She counted off on her fingers. 'We've had fingers glued together, an allergic reaction to the permanent marker she tried on her lips, a broken wrist from her trampoline and an X-ray for a dime she swallowed.'

Abigail's father continued to cringe. He shook his head. 'I know. I'm sorry. We can't seem to stay away.'

Avery opened up his hand. 'Well, today is something different. Today we have beads.'

Katsuko stared at the small multicoloured wooden beads in Avery's palm. She dreaded to ask.

'Can I have a set of alligator forceps, a set of bayonet forceps, a curved hook and a cerumen loop?' Katsuko gave a nod. It was the standard equipment that could be used to try and retrieve the variety of items that kids could stuff up their noses.

He pulled out a small pocket torch and spoke to Abigail. 'I'm just going to tilt your head back and see if I can see anything up there.'

Abigail gave a giggle. 'Red and purple,' she said happily.

Avery's eyes widened. 'You stuck a red and a purple bead up your nose?'

Her father rolled his eyes. 'This is what I'm up against.'

Katsuko had collected the equipment on the trolley and added a sterile dressing pack and gloves. She opened a nearby cupboard. 'Some phenylephrine?'

Avery gave a nod. She prepared the equipment and waited until he'd explained what he was going to do.

'Okay, Abigail. We can't leave those nasty beads up your nose. They could cause lots of trouble. So we need to try and get them back out.' He picked up some tissues. 'We'll start easy. I'm going to get you to blow your nose while I hold one side closed. It might feel a bit strange, but just try and blow as best you can.'

Katsuko watched patiently. He had a nice manner with Abigail. Her dad looked exasperated and she couldn't blame him—their ER was becoming a second home to the little girl.

Avery examined the contents of the tissues and shook his head. 'Okay, then, no beads. Let me have another look.'

He dropped to his knees again and checked with the torch. 'I can definitely see one of them. It shouldn't be too hard to reach. Let's try a little phenylephrine first—this helps stop any swelling,' he explained to Abigail's father.

Katsuko handed over the medicine and waited until he'd applied it. She gave him a little wink and nodded to the father. 'I expect First Lieutenant Bruce might want you to have a chat with Abigail while the medicine is working.'

Avery picked up on things quickly. 'You're absolutely right, Nurse. I'll do that.'

He knelt back down and held up the bayonet forceps. 'Abigail, I'm going to have to very gently put these inside your nose to pull out the beads. It won't hurt. You can stay on your dad's knee but I'll need you to stay very still. Can you do that for me?'

Abigail eyed the forceps suspiciously. They could be intimidating for kids, but Avery obviously believed in being straightforward.

Avery sat them back down. 'You've been here a few times now. Everyone can have an accident, but sticking things up your nose isn't really an accident. Neither is sticking your fingers together or deciding to put pen on your lips. You had an allergic reaction that time. That could have been dangerous.'

'I like it here,' Abigail said simply.

Avery straightened a little and glanced over at Katsuko.

He positioned Abigail back against her father's chest and got him to put one arm across her chest and the other on her forehead. 'Are you okay holding her?'

He gave a nod. 'I've had to do it before and I'm sure I'll have to do it again.'

Avery handed the torch to Katsuko, washed his hands and put on the gloves. 'I'm going to stick with the bayonet forceps. I think they will be best.'

He positioned himself in front of Abigail and her father and tilted Abigail's head back gently, letting Katsuko shine the torch. He spoke quietly and calmly. 'This will be over in a few seconds, just hold still.'

There was barely time to suck in a breath. Avery moved swiftly. The forceps were inserted, he grasped a bead and pulled steadily. There was a tinkle of the purple bead hitting the metal trolley. Abigail's eyes widened. 'You got it.'

Avery nodded. 'I got it. I'll give you a second then we'll have a look with the torch to see if I can see the red bead.'

'He got it, Daddy, he got it.'

Her father sighed and looked relieved. 'So he did.' He positioned Abigail back against his chest. 'Now, hold still and let's see if he can get the other one.'

Katsuko bent down and shone the torch for him again. Avery didn't hesitate. He saw the bead and had the forceps in swiftly. The red bead landed on the metal trolley with a satisfactory ping.

Avery set the forceps down, pulled the gloves from his hands and walked back over to the sink.

He signalled to Katsuko and she understood instantly. 'Lieutenant Bruce, can you come with me to fill in some paperwork?'

'Oh, okay.' He lifted Abigail from his knee and sat her up on the ER trolley, following Katsuko from the cubicle. She knew that Avery wanted a chance to talk to Abigail alone. It wasn't that she had any child protection concerns. She didn't get that vibe at all. But it was obvious that something was going on in the little girl's head and if Avery could get to the bottom of it, maybe it would stop the frequent ER visits.

She took him over to the desk. 'Chari, can Lieutenant Bruce get the paperwork he needs to fill in for his daughter, Abigail? And could you get him a coffee?'

Chari looked up from the desk and stood up, her telepathic powers working instantly. All of the staff in the ER were good at this kind of thing. Chari would know that Katsuko was stalling for time. She shot Katsuko a beaming smile. 'Absolutely, no problem. Come with me, Lieutenant Bruce.'

Katsuko nodded and headed back to the cubicle. She could hear Avery talking to Abigail and she paused outside to listen.

He was joking with her. 'So, you've been here quite a lot. What is it you like so much about this place?' He slapped his hand on his chest. 'It's me, isn't it?'

The little girl shook her head, looking from side to side. 'Don't be silly, it's not you. You just got here.'

Avery had moved her from the trolley to the chair but she jumped down and looked underneath the trolley.

'Is it the candy? Did you hear that some of the nurses carry candy for kids?'

Abigail frowned. 'Not all of them.' Then she smiled. 'But Frank does. He has Jelly Bears.' She'd moved over to the curtains separating the cubicles and was trying to peer around them.

Avery walked over the pulled the curtain back. There was no one in the next cubicle. 'Did you want to see something?'

Abigail walked over and bent down, looking under the other trolley, then shook her head and stood back up.

Katsuko couldn't help but grin. While her actions were curious, she was acting more like a little old lady than a kid.

Abigail pressed her lips together and looked carefully at Avery. 'Can I go over there?'

She was pointing to the cubicles at the other side of the bay. Now Katsuko was definitely intrigued.

Avery spoke gently to her. 'What are you looking for, Abigail?'

There was a long pause. It was clear she wasn't sure about replying. She looked around as if she was checking who was listening. 'I'm looking for my caterpillar,' she whispered.

'Your caterpillar?' Avery looked as confused as it was humanly possible to look.

'I had it with me when I fell off the trampoline. I lost it. I didn't remember until I got home.'

Katsuko smiled. Now things were starting to make sense.

'So why didn't you just ask someone to find it for you?'

The little girl pressed her lips together. 'It matched a book that Nanna bought me.'

'What was the book?'

'It was about a caterpillar. You could stick your finger

through the pages.' Katsuko nodded. She'd had the same book as a child. Most kids had probably had the same book.

Abigail's eyes filled with tears. 'Nanna's gone now. I can't tell Daddy I've lost her caterpillar. He'd be angry.'

Katsuko caught her breath. Things were becoming crystal clear. This was why Abigail had created a range of reasons to come back to the ER.

Avery shook his head and pulled Abigail up onto his knee. 'I don't think he would be, sweetheart. I think he's more worried about the fact you keep coming back here. Is that why you do it? You want to come and try to find your caterpillar?'

She nodded and he sighed. 'What say I speak to my favourite nurse and see if we can try and find your caterpillar?'

'Will she tell?' whispered Abigail.

'I can promise you she won't tell. She's very good at keeping secrets.'

Katsuko leaned back against the wall for a second. She could still just see them. He had a good way with kids. He knew how to engage with them and he knew the right questions to ask. Not all military docs could do that. Most of them were used to dealing with adults instead of kids. There was something so sexy about seeing a guy who was good around children.

Avery stood up and put Abigail back on the chair. 'Lieutenant Williams, are you around?'

She felt her chest swell a little. A tiny little part of her had hoped that he had been talking about her. But she hadn't really been sure.

She pulled back the curtain. 'Yes, Captain Flynn.'

He smiled at her. 'Do we have a lost property box here?'

She frowned. 'I think we might have. But I'm not sure if there's much in it. Do you want me to look for something?'

He glanced over at Abigail. 'Would you be able to check it for a caterpillar?'

Katsuko tried not to smile. She kept her face as straight as possible. 'And what does this caterpillar look like, Captain Flynn?'

He knelt down next to Abigail. 'Can you tell Katsuko what your caterpillar looks like?'

She nodded. 'It's green and yellow. And squishy. With a red face and purple...things.'

Katsuko touched Abigail's shoulder. 'Give me a second and I'll go and check.'

Avery shot her a grateful smile and it sent a little buzz right through her system as she walked down the corridor. It only took a few seconds to find the lost property box. Katsuko had a quick rummage through it. Umbrellas, hats, books and kids' jacket. There was even a single shoe. But no squishy caterpillars.

She sighed and bit her lip. There had to be a solution. She pulled out her phone and did a quick search. It didn't take long to find what she needed.

She smiled and stuck her phone back in her pocket, walking back to the cubicle. She ducked in behind the curtain, glancing between Avery and Abigail. The little girl was clutching her arms to her chest, waiting for the news.

Katsuko knelt down next to her and spoke carefully. 'I couldn't find the caterpillar, Abigail. I'm sorry.'

The little girl looked as though she might cry, and Katsuko put her hand over Abigail's. 'But I think I might know where I can get one.'

Abigail's eyes widened. 'You do?'

'You do?' Avery knelt down beside her and Katsuko almost laughed as she was hit by the overkill of his aftershave again. She pulled her phone out and turned it around.

'Does your caterpillar look like this, Abigail?'

The little girl let out a squeal. 'Yes! That's it. Where is it?'

Avery closed his hand over hers to take the phone. Tingles shot up her arm.

She met his gaze. Those pale green eyes fixed on her and she swallowed. It was almost as if the person who'd chosen their obligatory green scrubs had picked the exact shade of his eyes. She'd never seen green eyes quite that pale before. It was making her think a whole lot of thoughts she shouldn't about a guy she hardly knew. A guy who seemed to flirt for fun.

Thing was, flirting back was kind of fun. And when was the last time she'd done that?

'There's a bookshop nearby that sells a boxed set with the book and toy together. I'm sure we'll be able to find one.'

Abigail gasped. 'There's another caterpillar?'

Avery smiled and leaned forward. He whispered, 'What if I promise that I'll buy you another caterpillar? If I can get you one and Katsuko brings it around, would you stop finding reasons to come to the ER?'

Abigail nodded solemnly, her eyes wide.

'Is everything okay?' They both turned towards the voice. Abigail's father was standing at the curtains. 'Can I take her home?'

Avery nodded. 'Of course you can. We've had a little chat about Abigail's visits to the ER. Here's hoping we won't see you again for quite a while.'

Abigail's dad looked a bit confused but he nodded and picked up Abigail. 'Come on, mischief. Let's get you home.'

Avery leaned against the wall and watched father and daughter go down the hall. He was smiling that dopey smile again.

She'd need to watch out. He was beginning to do strange things to her normally rational mind. The last thing she wanted to do was let her guard down. Not with an American. Not with someone who would disappear in a few months when he was reassigned. Fitting in around here was hard enough, without becoming the talk of the base by dating a co-worker.

A gentle nudge at her waist brought her out of her thoughts. He was looking very pleased with himself. 'You know what this means, don't you?'

She shook her head. Her stomach was starting to rumble and it was definitely time for coffee. 'No. What does it mean?'

'It means we have a date.' He glanced at his watch. 'And it starts in five hours.'

CHAPTER FOUR

SHE APPEARED AT his door within an hour of them finishing their shifts. She wrinkled her nose as she walked inside. 'What did you do?'

He shook his head. 'What didn't I do? I've used every air freshener on the base, I've tried industrial-strength cleaner… This place was borderline cold last night because of the amount of windows I had to open.'

He lifted his T-shirt from his chest and smelled it. 'I'm just worried that the smell will start to permeate me. If I start to smell like this place you need to tell me.'

She laughed. 'Believe me, if you start to smell like this place I'll be nowhere near you.'

He picked up his fedora and stuck it on his head. 'Well, we can't have that, can we?'

'Are you really going to wear that?'

'I told you. It's a family heirloom. Can't leave home without it.'

She'd thought he'd been joking before, but now it seemed he was serious.

'There has to be a story there.'

He shrugged. 'There might be.'

He opened his front door and picked up his keys. 'This will be my first time off base. My first time in Japan—

my first experience of Tokyo. What do you have planned for me?'

She felt a mild sense of panic. She hadn't even thought about anything like that. Normally, if she had friends visiting from abroad she'd plan a whole host of things for them to do. When new people started at the base she'd sometimes take them on a city tour, or at least sit down with them and make some recommendations.

'I'd only planned on taking you to a book store. What do you have in mind?' She walked out the door ahead of him.

He closed the door behind them and fell into step beside her. She was conscious of the fact that anyone who saw them would realise they were going off base together. It was no big deal. None. So why did it bother her?

'How about you try some sushi this time? Or some karaoke?' She let out a laugh. 'Or maybe I'll introduce you to a *sento* or an *onsen*.'

He looked at her curiously. 'What do you mean?'

She waved her hand. 'No. I'll save that for another day.' A breeze swept by them, giving her another dose of his aftershave.

She stopped walking. 'That's what we'll do.'

'What?'

'We'll go somewhere you can find some new aftershave. You smell like all the teenage boys around here when they've stolen some of their father's aftershave for the first time.'

He lifted an eyebrow at her. 'That bad, eh?' She almost laughed out loud. The move, and the line delivery was almost like something from a movie.

There was something about this guy that was so infectious. Most of the staff had been talking about him today. They were impressed by his quick actions the day before and his clinical skills. There had been the inevitable discussion about his good looks and whether he was attached or not. Then there had been a few comments about the fact that he seemed to have homed in on the Major General's daughter already.

Those comments had made her distinctly uncomfortable. She was almost sure that he hadn't known initially—no one did. But by the time he'd asked her to show him where to eat he *had* known.

Part of that made her skin prickle. She'd like to think that who her father was didn't matter to him, but she really didn't know him that well yet.

It didn't help that the first thing she'd noticed had been how well his dark blue jeans fitted around his backside, or that the thin designer T-shirt showed the definition of his pecs.

She almost jumped when he slung his arm around her shoulders and pulled her closer. 'Hey? Where are you?'

She stopped walking. 'What?'

'You looked a million miles away. You had a strange expression on your face. Everything okay?'

She stepped out from under his arm. He'd already got too close.

'I'm fine.' She gave herself a shake as they approached the base exit and held out her arm. 'Here we are, the prefecture of Tokyo.'

'Don't you mean city?'

She shook her head. 'Tokyo isn't a city. It's a prefecture. It has twenty-three wards, twenty-six cities, five towns and eight villages. Not to mention the two island chains. It's the most populous metropolis in the world.' She laughed and said, 'We could stand here all day and argue about the size of the population.'

His eyes widened. 'Wow.'

She nodded as they left the base. 'Let's head to the subway. It's the quickest way to get to where we want to go.'

'You've still not told me where we're going or what we're doing.'

She gave a little shudder. 'Feel free to pile the pressure on. There's a million things to do in Tokyo. But most of them have to be planned. I could take you to Shibuya's shopping district and the famous Hachiko crossing.'

This time he gave a shudder. 'Not tonight.'

She smiled as they bought tickets for the subway. 'What about the Imperial Palace? Or the Meiji Shrine? Do you like the outdoors? We could visit the Japanese Gardens. Or plan for another day and go on the bullet train or visit Mount Fuji.'

The subway was fast and efficient and only took a few minutes to appear. 'Sounds like there's too much to do in Tokyo.'

She nodded. 'There is. Whatever it is you want to find, I'm pretty sure I'll be able to find it. You just need to plan. Tokyo and its districts are a big place. It would take around two and a half hours to get to Mount Fuji from here.'

Avery fixed his eyes on the snow-topped peak in the distance. 'It looks fantastic. I'd love to go there one day.' He met her gaze and smiled as the subway rolled along. The shudder of the subway echoed the shudder in her body. The smile seemed genuine. He seemed a warm and friendly guy. But did she really want to get involved with someone she worked with?

Wow. Where had that thought come from?

He reached up and put his hand on her shoulder. Touch. He seemed to be big on touch.

'But from the list you gave me there's a whole lot of Tokyo out there. Seems like I'll be spending most of my time off exploring the place.'

Someone jostled her from behind and she stumbled forward a little, pressing right up against Avery's chest. She looked up. 'Sorry.'

He put his hand on her hip. 'It's fine. It seems really busy around here. I guess we should just get used to being up close and personal.'

It was the way he'd said it. Half joking, half serious. She wasn't quite sure which. And she wasn't quite sure which one she wanted.

She pressed her lips together and gave him a nudge. 'Get ready to wrestle your way out of here. The next stop is ours.'

Three minutes later they were standing in front of the multi-storey bookshop. 'I thought these places had gone out of fashion. Doesn't everyone read on phones these days?'

She gave him a shocked glance. 'Shame on you. There's nothing nicer than the smell of a brand-new book. Don't you just love the way they feel in your hands? Can't you remember the excitement of being a kid and been taken to a bookstore and told to pick what you wanted?'

He had an amused expression on his face, with tiny crinkles around his eyes. He glanced upwards at the huge store, which had windows lined with books. 'I can't say that I did. I was more a racing-track and cars kind of kid.'

They walked through the main entrance and she shot him a curious glance. 'You mean you didn't have a mini-stethoscope and medical kit?'

He shook his head as she pointed at the escalator towards the kids' books. 'No way. I didn't want to be a doctor then.'

She turned to face him as they rode up the escalator. 'Really? What did you want to be?'

He tipped his hat at her. 'Can't you tell?'

'No way. You wanted to be Indiana Jones?'

'Doesn't every small boy?'

She reached up and touched his hat. 'I thought you said it was a family heirloom? Oops!'

He grabbed her arm as she fell backwards. She'd been so engrossed in quizzing Avery that she'd forgotten the escalator would reach the top quickly. But his timing wasn't so good. As she fell back she pulled him with her and they both landed on the floor at the top of the elevator, Avery flat on top of her.

A teenage boy with wide eyes stepped over them as Avery rolled her to the side.

'We've got to stop meeting like this,' he groaned.

He was squished right up against her. She'd thought they'd been close on the subway. But now she could feel every one of his tight muscles pressed against her. She could actually feel the beat of his heart against her chest. She didn't even want to think too hard about anything else she could feel.

She pushed back and scrambled to her feet. 'Sorry, I should have been paying attention. I got distracted. It's just that—'

He stood up next to her and shook his head. 'We're fine, Katsuko. You're babbling.'

Her reaction was instant. She wrinkled her nose and put her hands on her hips. 'I am not.'

Her cheeks started to flush. Maybe she had been babbling just a little. He grabbed her hand. 'Come on. Let's find the kids' books. There has to be a caterpillar in here somewhere.'

She was trying not to focus on the fact that his hand was encircling hers. She was trying to completely ignore the tiny sparks that were shooting up her arm directly into her chest.

The kids' section had huge signs hanging above it—some in Japanese and some in English. It didn't take long to find the children's picture books. They had a number of little sets and the caterpillar book was among them. Avery smiled as he picked it up. 'She was right, you know. Mainly green and yellow with a red face and purple...things.'

Katsuko laughed. 'That would be antennae, Captain Flynn.'

'Yeah, yeah. Well, I'm a doctor, not a vet.'

She frowned for a second. 'So how come you're so good with kids? You said you don't have any of your own—does someone in your family have kids? Are you really Avery, the fun uncle?' She was curious.

He gave a visible shudder.

'What?'

He gave his head a shake. 'Thankfully, my sister doesn't have kids.' He put his hand on his chest. 'I do however, have a number of good friends who have children. In fact, two of my friends seem to be having a competition of fitting in the most number of kids under the age of five.' He raised his eyebrows. 'It's currently a draw.'

'How many kids do they actually have?' She was leaving the sister comment, even though she was still curious. It was clear that was for another day.

'Tess and Ray have four—a set of twins of eight months, a son of two and a son of four. Jamal and Aiysha have four too. They're like stepping stones. Four, three, two and one.'

'And what are you, chief babysitter?'

He gave her a beaming smile and nodded. 'Of course I am. It helps that I'm a big kid myself. Letting any of them get a few hours for dinner, or an evening to themselves, is no big deal. It might take me a few days to recover but it's worth it.'

He pulled some money from his pocket. 'How are you going to get this to Abigail?'

She thought for a few seconds. 'It should be easy enough. I'll just take it out of the box and pretend I found it in the ER and wondered if it was hers. It's almost true.'

He paid for the boxed set and they walked back to the escalators. He gave her a wicked smile and gestured towards the moving stairs. 'After you. Don't want to land on you again.'

She stepped onto the escalator and turned to face him

again. 'What if I like living dangerously?' She leaned back a little and held her hands up as they travelled downwards. 'Hey, look at me, I'm going to fall. Woo...!' She gave him a cheeky wink. 'Don't worry, you're safe. I knocked you down and now you did the same to me. I think we're even.' She spun around just as they reached the bottom and stepped off sharply.

'I'm not sure we're even,' murmured Avery. 'I'm sure both times it was your fault.' He had a mischievous gleam in his eye that she'd no intention of falling for.

She planted her hands on her hips as they walked back out into the crowds. Darkness had fallen and Tokyo was lit up with a whole array of coloured lights. 'What kind of gratitude is that? You drag me out after a busy shift to take you shopping and introduce you to life in Tokyo, then you hit me with the guilt trip?'

He kept going. 'I'm just pointing out that you seem to like me flat on my back.' For a second she was mesmerised. Those pale green eyes were quite startling under the brown fedora and bathed by neon lights. The noise and bustle around her seemed to dull. All she could feel right now was the electricity in the air between them. It didn't matter that he was teasing. It didn't matter that his blatant flirting was ridiculous.

She liked it. She could feel herself start to react it. To flirt back. She was comfortable around him. Already, in the space of two days.

She bit the inside of her cheek. She could tell that shopping wasn't really his thing. But she wasn't ready to go home yet. Her phone buzzed and she pulled it out of her pocket, glanced at the message and quickly pushed it back in her jeans. Her grandmother. Not what she needed right now. 'How about I promise you somewhere really cool to go and eat genuine Japanese sushi?'

'Now, that does sound tempting. Do you promise not to get me flat on my back again?'

'Not unless you want me to.' It came out before she thought about it. Like a lightning flash in her brain that reached her lips before the mute part of her brain started to function.

He raised his eyebrows. 'Oh, touché, First Lieutenant Williams.'

'Touché? What's that?'

He waved his hand. 'Never mind. Tell me more about where we're going to get some food.'

She gave him a knowing smile. 'Well, strangely enough, it's right next to one of the main tourist attractions.'

'Which one?'

'The one you're most excited about seeing. Come on, it's just a quick jump on the subway.'

Ten minutes later Avery found himself in the middle of a film set. At least, that was what it looked like and felt like.

He'd never seen so many people before. The sun had set quickly and darkness had fallen across Tokyo. The whole street was lit up by the biggest array of neon lights he'd ever seen. It reminded him partly of Times Square and partly of a futuristic film.

But the thing that was most noticeable was the number of people in one area. He'd never seen a busier place in his life.

Yes, he'd realised that Tokyo was busy. It was the most populated place in the world—of course it would be busy.

But as they exited Shibuya station he had a sudden realisation that he'd never truly understood the definition of busy before. He spent every second step stopping to avoid crashing into someone.

Katsuko, on the other hand, moved nimbly and ably through the throngs of people. His eyes were repeatedly drawn to her neat bum in the bright red skinny jeans. She pointed to the crossing before them. 'Watch out because when the lights turn red they turn red everywhere. People just surge forward onto the road. Keep close or you'll get lost.'

He resisted the temptation to reach out and grab her hand. He'd made a few close moves around her and got the distinct impression she wasn't quite sure what to make of them. Truth was, neither was he.

It felt natural to touch Katsuko—even though he'd no right to, or had any invitation to. If he'd been challenged about it, he'd claim he touched all his female friends. It was casual. It was friendly. But the buzz that flooded his body every time he came into contact with her skin was telling him a whole other story.

Would it be fine to date the General's daughter? Or would it be frowned upon? Because in the space of two days those thoughts were definitely starting to float around his mind.

She seemed fun. She was good at her job. And she knew the area like the back of her hand. She bordered on flirtatious without being forward.

It didn't matter that he never settled anywhere. It didn't matter that his longest relationship had only lasted the length of time of his posting.

His family was the best ever example of things not lasting for ever. With a father who'd married four times, and was about to move on to number five, a mother who latched onto the nearest guy with money until she'd spent it all, and a sister who was learning from her mother's example, it was no wonder he didn't do any kind of family gatherings.

His last stepmother had been a woman only a few years older than him and she had insisted on inviting him around at New Year. The last New Year's dinner had been a complete disaster. His father had got horribly drunk, insulted just about everyone sitting around the dinner table, then passed out on the sofa.

Never. Ever. Again.

He hadn't even told any of them his orders had changed and he was in Japan now. They probably wouldn't care.

The only person he'd really respected in the family had been the owner of the fedora—his uncle Stu. He'd been a real life Indiana Jones, disappearing into parts of the continents that no one had heard of and coming back with artefacts for the museum he'd worked for and a whole host of fantastic stories.

Because he'd been a kid, Avery hadn't really understood the politics of it all—or the danger. All he'd known was that Uncle Stu had been shot at a few times, been threatened on occasion and had had to run from a bunch of robbers in more than one set of circumstances.

It had been very exciting for a young boy. Right up until the point an official-looking letter had been delivered to the door and his father had disappeared for a few days, returning with only the fedora. 'It seemed Uncle Stuey took the wrong artefact' was all he'd said before he'd dumped the fedora onto Avery's head and disappeared into his study.

Avery had been lost. Uncle Stu—crazy as he'd been—had been the most normal person in the family. They'd joked about working together when he was old enough to join his uncle on the expeditions. It had never occurred to him that might never happen.

Nothing else in the world had seemed certain after that.

Joining the air force had been the steadiest part of his life. Stu had left him a little money that he'd used to part pay for college and medical school. With no family or home to support back in the US he was now almost debt free. A great position to be in.

Why shouldn't he date the woman he wanted to?

As they darted among the crowds, recognition dawned

in his brain. This time he did reach for her hand and tugged it. 'Hey, this is that place, isn't it?'

She gave him her most innocent expression. 'What place?'

He wrinkled his nose. 'I can't remember what you called it. *Ha*-something—the crazy crossing?'

People all around them had their phones in the air, ready to capture the moment that the lights changed. A few seconds later it happened. And it seemed like the whole world moved.

'Watch out!' said Katsuko as she pulled him back against the wall of a building.

It would be so easy to get swept along with the momentum of the crowd. He climbed up a few steps to get a better view. 'Wow.' It was almost like a form of dancing or synchronised swimming. And it wasn't slow—it was fast. People dodged around each other instantly, heading in all directions. Some moved in straight lines, some diagonally.

'How do they do that?' he wondered out loud.

Katsuko smiled at him and shrugged. 'What can I say? We're naturals. Welcome to Hachiko crossing—the busiest crossing in the world.'

As the throng of people disappeared quickly the lights changed again. Within a few seconds people started to accumulate at the sidewalks all over again.

He folded his arms and faced her. 'You mentioned this place and I said not tonight.' He was still gazing in wonder. 'I didn't expect it to be quite like this.'

'Well, get used to it. The place we're going for dinner is diagonal to us.' She pointed to a silver and blue high-rise building. 'Are you chicken?'

'What?'

He finally dragged his eyes off the crossing to face her. There was no doubt about it. There was a definite smirk on her face. She was baiting him. Again.

'You think I'm chicken?'

She leaned forward, as if their conversation could be heard by others. 'I think you're a Hachiko virgin. Let's just call it survival of the fittest here.' Her voice was low and he had to move closer to hear. Somehow he knew it was a deliberate act. And the choice of words?

He didn't have a single doubt that over the next few months Katsuko Williams was going to drive him crazy. Good crazy.

'Do you want to take a bet on this?'

She looked at him curiously. 'And what exactly would that bet be?'

He liked it. She'd take the bet, whatever it was.

'Who can get across quicker?'

She laughed out loud. 'Are you crazy? You, the slow-moving, never-been-here-before American, against me, the agile local girl?'

Every word made his skin prickle. He loved her feistiness. He loved the challenge in her eyes. He glanced over at the throng with his chin held high. He could hardly see any gaps between all the bodies. 'I played American football. That's not a crowd. That's just a smooth path to home.'

She shook her head. He could tell from her expression that she thought she'd already won. She waved her hand. 'I guess it doesn't matter, but what do I win?'

A group of rowdy workers passed by, singing at the tops of their voices. 'A kiss,' he said suddenly.

He'd touched her. He could smell her. But he wanted to taste her. Taste those lips.

Her brow furrowed and she pulled back a little. 'Not a chance.' She was surprised but she didn't seem repelled. Although she might flirt with him and taunt him a little, there was still a whole host of invisible barriers surrounding her. She put her hands back on her hips. 'Loser has to buy dinner. That seems fair.'

She gave a flick of her shiny geometric-styled hair. It seemed to all move together. There was never a hair out of place. What would she look like if it was all mussed up? He was beginning to realise that that move seemed to indicate she'd made up her mind. 'I still plan on collecting that kiss,' he murmured under his breath.

She took a few steps in front of him and he grabbed the back of her black fitted jacket before she disappeared into the crowd completely. By the time they reached the edge of the crossing people were packed around them. He tucked his head on her shoulder and stood right up close. He had the perfect excuse. There was no space around them at all.

He pointed diagonally across the street. 'That building over there? That's where we're headed?'

She nodded. 'Twenty-second floor has one of the best sushi restaurants around. We can sit and watch the madness of the crossing.'

'Sounds good.' He glanced upwards. He could sense the people around him leaning forward a little, ready to move the second the lights changed. He lowered his mouth to her ear. 'See you at the front doors.'

He couldn't wipe the smile from his face as he darted out from behind her, making a beeline for the building. Once he was in the middle of the thing it wasn't quite so daunting. The Japanese people were endearingly polite. They seemed to have a sixth sense for stepping out of the way—in the right direction. The only blips on the horizon were the number of crazy tourists who were standing in the middle of the crossing, holding their phones above their heads and filming. Didn't they realise as soon as the traffic lights changed colour they could be squashed by oncoming traffic?

He couldn't see Katsuko anywhere. But how on earth would he in this crowd? He kept his eyes on the prize, the glass doors, now just in front of him. If the crossing had been empty, it would probably have taken around twenty seconds to run from where they'd started to their final destination. But the sea of people made that impossible. How long would the lights actually stay on red?

He dodged out of the way of a few more people. Any second now he would be dizzy with the amount of zigzagging he was doing. But the prize would be worth it. He would pay for dinner no matter what. What he really wanted was the kiss.

The crowd thinned a little as he approached the faraway sidewalk. There, standing with an amused expression on her face and her arms crossed, was Katsuko. She looked as if she'd been there for a while.

'What?' He glanced behind him and back to her again. Yep, it was definitely her. Red skinny jeans, black T-shirt embellished with sparkling sequins in the neon lights and a cropped black leather jacket. She was laughing now.

He thudded in front of her, pretending not to be breathless. 'How on earth did you do that? Where did you come from?'

She kept laughing as she spun around and the automatic doors slid open in front of them. 'You'll have to be here twenty-five years to keep up with me.'

He still couldn't believe it. The lights had changed behind them and the crossing was instantly filled with traffic. She walked over and pressed the button at the elevators. 'I'm going to have the most expensive thing on the menu.' She glanced at him sideways as they stepped inside. 'And I might even have some wine.'

'You can have as much wine as you like. I still want to know how you did that. Is it a trick?'

'What? Like you trying to get a quick getaway?'

The elevator slid smoothly upwards. He was smarting. He was thinking about that kiss a lot more than he should. It might have sounded like a joke. But it wasn't really. A bet had seemed simple. A way to get permission to kiss her. And right now he wanted that way more than he should.

The doors slid open at the twenty-second floor and they stepped out to a restaurant that had glass panels all around. There was a perfect view of the Shibuya shopping district with all its chaos.

Avery checked the queue of people ahead of them. 'I take it this is a popular place, then?'

She nodded. 'Once you've been you'll want to come back. Guaranteed.'

He looked at the queue ahead. Even though the restaurant had gorgeous views—particularly of the crossing below—people didn't seem to stay long. Their orders were taken, then they slid along a bench in front of the chefs as their meal was prepared. Once they reached the end they picked up their plate and took it to one of the tables to eat. Most of the sushi dishes were prepared within a few minutes so the queue moved along swiftly. He was kind of amused that the people seemed to eat their dishes equally quickly then leave. There was no lingering over a meal like most Europeans and Americans did. The Japanese didn't seem to waste any time anywhere.

Katsuko turned to face him. 'What do you want to eat?'

He made a face. 'To be honest, I'm not really sure. Although I've eaten in Japanese restaurants all over the world, I've never been in one in Japan before. What do you recommend?'

'Is there anything you don't like?'

He gave her a taunting smile. 'I'm pretty much a guy who'll try anything.'

She rolled her eyes. 'You never stop, do you?' She gave a shake of her head and stuck her hands on her hips. 'It's going to get old, you know.'

She pointed at a nearby menu. 'I'd recommend starting with some *nigiri* and some miso soup.' He smiled. *Nigiri* was one of the basics. A slice of raw fish pressed over some vinegared rice. 'Then my favourite from here are the fatty *chu-toro*—that's tuna—super-soft *aori ika*—that's squid—and fresh, local *aji*—that's mackerel with ginger and *negi*.'

Avery nodded. 'All sounds good to me. You're the expert here. I'm just happy to watch the cooking and get eating.' They ordered drinks at the bar and Katsuko sipped her wine as she spoke rapid Japanese to the chefs. They slid along the cream leather bench and watched in fascination as the chefs expertly sliced, chopped and prepared food. The preparation time was minimal. These guys were complete and utter professionals. Avery pointed to one small plate of food with a few *nigiri*. 'That would probably take me hours to prepare,' he said to Katsuko as he took a drink from his beer. 'I think I could watch them all day.'

'I couldn't,' she said quickly. 'I just want to eat.'

As they slid along the bench, following their food being finished, Avery was fascinated with the whole experience. When the food was plated they carried it over to a table overlooking the Hachiko crossing. He had used chopsticks before but just wasn't very good with them. Katsuko laughed at his efforts and leaned over to reposition them in his hands, her warm skin touching his.

'Watch out, Katsuko,' he warned with a smile. 'I'll think you're trying to deliberately touch me.'

'I'm trying to stop your food landing in your lap,' she said smartly.

He ate for a few minutes, looking down in awe at the still crowded crossing. It was teeming with people and after a few minutes they started pointing out the people they thought would never reach the other side in time. It was almost like a kids' game.

'This food is delicious. You're right. I will come here again.'

She nodded. 'It helps to eat it just after it's prepared.

Sushi should be eaten at the optimal fish and rice temperature. It tastes best then.'

He noticed a few of the other men around glancing in her direction. Katsuko was bright and lively. It didn't hurt that she was the prettiest woman in the room with a whole lot of sexy thrown in there too.

'Who texted you earlier? Was it an admirer? I bet you've got a few on base.'

She didn't flinch at all. 'Nope. No admirer. It was my grandmother.'

'Your grandmother? You mentioned her before. How is she?'

'Still here.'

He was surprised by her blunt answer. 'What does that mean?'

She took a deep breath. 'Let's just say I've always had the distinct impression that my mother and subsequently me are the biggest embarrassments of her life. In fact, it's not really an impression at all. It's fact. She's said it.'

'She what?' It seemed like such a harsh thing to say. And even though Katsuko said it so matter-of-factly there was no hiding the glimmer of hurt in her dark brown eyes. His insides automatically coiled upwards.

Katsuko took a sip of her wine. She was trying so hard to appear indifferent. Did she know she couldn't look indifferent no matter how hard she tried?

He reached over and touched her hand. 'Tell me more about your grandmother.'

He was definitely curious. There was a story there. But he was more curious at Katsuko's reaction to her grandmother's text.

She shrugged. 'What's to tell? I see her when I have to, which isn't often as she doesn't particularly like me. She wants the whole world to jump for her. I've learned the hard way not to do it. The more I get involved the more I get hurt. Adulthood has taught me to move into self-protect mode.'

He didn't know quite what to say. Lots of families were fractured, lots of families were broken. His own wasn't ideal. But this? This was a whole other story. Was her grandmother her only living relative?

'Do you have other family in Japan? Aunts, uncles, cousins?'

She shook her head. There was an air of sadness about her. 'No. My mother was an only child. I think my grandmother had some cousins once, but I'm sure she treated them the same way she treats everyone else.'

'And how is that?'

She met his gaze square on. 'With disdain. With disapproval.'

He released her hand and leaned back in his chair a little. 'Those are harsh words.'

'She's a harsh woman.'

He signalled to the waiter.

'What are you doing?'

He gave a rueful smile. 'I'm ordering us more drinks. I don't care if we're supposed to eat and run in here. I want to know more.'

She bit her lip and he wondered if he was pushing her more than he should. But she'd been the one to mention it, and he wanted to know more about her. He gave her a moment as she pulled something from her bag. Her lips were still perfectly red but she slicked something over them that gave a waft of strawberries. He could sense delaying tactics easily.

He tapped his fingers on the table. 'Your grandmother must be quite modern.'

Katsuko let out something resembling a snort, then covered her face in embarrassment. 'I don't think anyone would describe my grandmother as modern.'

He held up his hands. 'She's texting. She must own a mobile phone. What age is she?'

'She's just over eighty. My mother was a late baby. She thought she couldn't have any children.'

'Then she must have been delighted when your mother came along.'

Katsuko sighed. 'You'd think so. But I think she'd got used to having no children. She'd accepted her fate. My mother was a shock. I don't think she ever really adjusted to having to replan her life.'

Avery pried a little further. 'You said she was unwell—she's in a wheelchair?'

Katsuko nodded. 'Her rheumatoid arthritis has been severe for as long as I've known her. She's been in a wheelchair since I was tiny. Her muscles are wasted. She has fibrosis of her lungs and kidney problems too. Every joint is affected. Her fingers are all disfigured. She doesn't use a phone. She uses a tablet.'

'Who takes care of her?'

Katsuko swallowed and glanced out of the window towards the busy crossing. A classic avoidance technique if ever he'd seen one.

'She has help.' Katsuko bit her lip again. She seemed annoyed.

'What kind of help does she need?'

Her gaze was fierce. She was obviously regretting this conversation. 'Every kind of help. Someone washes her, dresses her, prepares her food and amuses her for the day until they have to do it all again in reverse.'

Avery's brain was spinning. He wasn't quite sure of the healthcare system in Japan. Who helped when someone needed care at home?

But Katsuko didn't even let him ask the question. 'I pay for it. Don pays for it. She wouldn't let us help her. She told us in no uncertain terms.'

There it was again. That flicker of hurt. That deep-seated resentment.

'Why on earth does your grandmother treat you that way?'

Katsuko rested her elbows on the table and ran her hand through her shiny hair. She glanced around the restaurant, looking at the other people around them. She straightened in her seat and looked at him. 'Do you see anyone who looks like me?'

He frowned and looked around. Was it a trick question? 'Of course. There are lots of Japanese people in here.'

She shook her head. 'Look again. Look hard. Do you see anyone who looks like me?'

If this was test, he was going to fail.

'I don't know what you mean.'

She sighed and held up her hands. 'In Japan, I'm known as *hafu*—it's the term we use for biracial.' She glanced over her shoulder. 'I can't see anyone else in here that looks like me. Japan is one of the least ethnically diverse countries in the world. Some people think that people like me—*hafu*—aren't fully Japanese. My grandmother has always felt that.'

He was more than a little stunned. All he could see when he looked at Katsuko was her beauty. He hadn't thought much deeper than that. Oh, sure, when he'd first seen her he'd been a little curious. But that was all.

Working in the air force all around the world meant that race had never really been an issue for him to consider. His life had been full of people with varied nationalities and more mixed genetics than he could ever imagine.

He chose his words carefully. 'What does Don say about this?'

She sucked in her cheeks. 'Oh, Don is mad. Don has always been mad about the way she treats me. He was mad long before my mother and father died. When I was younger, he took me to visit her every two weeks. But he sat outside in the car for two hours, then knocked on the door to pick me up again. I gather they exchanged words during the custody issues—but neither of them has ever spoken about it.' She glanced out at the street again. 'When I turned eighteen, he told me it was up to me if I wanted to visit. I could drive by then. He just let me know he wouldn't force me to go.'

Avery tilted his head to the side. 'Was he trying to stop you going?'

'I don't think so. I think he'd just felt some sort of duty up until then. In Japan, you're not officially an adult until you're twenty. But I think Don's patience had worn thin by that point. I'd already been accepted for nursing. He told me it was up to me to decide what I wanted to do.'

Avery was watching her closely. She liked to keep things guarded, as if she held them close to her chest. Oh, she was talking. But years of being in the medical profession had frequently taught him that it wasn't what was said that was important—it was what *wasn't* said.

'What did you do?'

Her eyes fixed on the table. 'I visit when I can.'

'And you don't want to?'

Her fingers slid up and down the stem of the wine glass. 'Not really.' Her voice was barely a whisper.

He reached over. This time he didn't squeeze her hand. This time his fingers interlocked with hers. 'She doesn't know how lucky she is to have you.'

Her deep brown eyes met his and he could see her swallow. It was odd how he understood the awkwardness of family. The not-quite-fitting-in part. Their circumstances were completely different. But strangely similar. She'd lived here her whole life. He'd spent most of his adult life flitting around.

But the connection between them was real.

He hated the fact that she looked unhappy. 'Surely there must be lots of people on the base who are *hafu*?'

She nodded. 'On the base there are quite a few. I don't think there's anyone else that's Japanese and African-American, though. I guess I stand out a little because of the colour of my skin.'

'And that causes problems?'

She shrugged. 'It depends entirely on where you are. My mother wanted me to attend the same Japanese school that she did instead of a school on the base. But after a year of my being bullied for being "different" she changed her mind. I had some interviews at universities before I decided on becoming a nurse. Some of them were awkward. They asked me outright where I fitted. A lot of Japanese companies are very traditional. In a way, I think they were trying to prepare me for the adult working world. The truth is, even with a university degree, I might have found it difficult to find a job. The base is really the only place that makes me feel comfortable.'

Avery's brain was spinning. She looked so sad when she spoke that it was clear these experiences had really affected her. Who did she have to talk to about them?

The city he'd lived in as a child had people of every nationality—as did most of the bases he'd worked on. What he really wanted to do right now was hug her. She looked like she needed one. Instead, he leaned forward. 'Just for the record, I think you're pretty much perfect just the way you are.'

She rolled her eyes. 'You're flirting again.'

'Of course I am. I'm with the prettiest woman in the room. I'd be a fool not to.'

He couldn't help it. Katsuko could give blasé and smart answers. She was good at that. He'd thought before she was just sparky. Now he was realising it was part of the barriers she erected around herself. Self-protection.

He recognised them. He just wasn't ready to tell her why.

In his head, part of him was already walking away. No matter how much bravado she had, Katsuko wasn't the kind of woman he wanted to toy with.

He wasn't planning on being around her. He couldn't give her what she really needed. Someone to stand by her side. Someone to tell her how beautiful she was, and how good she was. He wasn't sure he could ever be that person.

The thing was, it didn't stop him wanting her.

In fact, it just magnified it.

No matter how wrong it was, he knew exactly what he'd do next.

He stood up. 'Let's go. There's something I want to do before we go back to the base.'

She gave a little start and made a grab for her jacket as he signalled to the waiter and settled the bill.

'No. Wait. Let me pay for part of that.'

He waved his hand. 'You can buy dessert.' He waited until she'd slid her arms into her jacket, then took her hand, leading her towards the elevator. There was already a crowd waiting and space was tight.

He smiled all the way down in the elevator, keeping her hand in his.

'What are we doing?'

He bent his head. 'Let's just say I'm still a tourist and I'm living the dream. Hachiko Crossing just made my bucket list.'

Outside it was even busier than before. The streets looked even more magical with their bright neon lights and flashing signs. They joined the crowd waiting to cross.

His thumb brushed against the inside of her palm. She gave him a curious smile. The lights changed and he shouted, 'Run!'

The shocked expression on her face was priceless. He wasn't quite sure how he managed it, but they darted in and out of the crowd without any injuries to either of them. As they approached the midway point of the crossing he stopped dead. Katsuko barrelled straight into the back of him. 'What?'

He spun around. They were dead centre. Exactly where he wanted to be.

A few eyebrows rose from people who sidestepped around them.

'What are you doing? Are you crazy? We need to cross before the lights change.'

Katsuko's head was darting from side to side. Time was running out.

But not for Avery.

He caught her head between both his hands. Her hair shone in the neon lights and her eyes sparkled. 'This is what I'm doing,' he said as he bent down and caught her perfect strawberry lips in his.

He felt her breath catch. But she was only rigid for the tiniest moment. One second later her body relaxed against his. Her lips were soft, pliable and seemed like they were moulded just for his.

His hands moved from her cheeks and tangled through her silky-soft hair. He could smell her. He could smell the perfume she was wearing, the shampoo from her hair and the strawberry from her lip gloss. He'd be happy if he could just stay here all night, inhaling her essence.

Her hands moved up to his shoulders, her fingers brushing against the skin at the side of his neck.

Reactions. That was just what he needed. Right in the middle of the busiest crossing in the world.

But somehow he knew Katsuko could cause this reaction in him anywhere.

There was a shout near them. She jumped back, pulling her lips from his.

The crowd had virtually disappeared around them, the

last few stragglers reaching the far sidewalk. 'Come on!' she shouted with a flash of panic.

For a second he wanted to object. To tell the world that his only priority right now was to get his lips back on hers.

But any second now they would resemble two squashed bugs.

He grabbed her hand and ran, sprinting as fast as they could towards the further sidewalk. He was laughing now. He couldn't help it. The whole thing was so ridiculous. It had flashed into his head in the restaurant, an overwhelming urge to have their first kiss in the middle of the monumental crossing.

People parted around them, amused expressions on their faces.

Avery and Katsuko bent over, both gasping for breath. She was laughing now too. 'What on earth were you thinking? Are you completely crazy?'

He shook his head as he caught his breath. There was something else in her eyes now. A sparkle that hadn't been there before. The sadness that had been there in the restaurant had vanished and he didn't ever want to see it again.

For a few minutes he pushed away his doubts about whether he could give her what she needed. This was all about the here and now.

He was still laughing. He straightened up and grabbed hold of her wrist again, pulling her over to the side of the street and into a doorway. 'I must be completely crazy.' He couldn't wipe the smile from his face. 'Because I'm going to do this again.'

And he did.

CHAPTER FIVE

HER SKIN FELT ITCHY, as if it prickled when she walked down the corridor at work.

She'd never felt self-conscious at work before. She could see her colleagues standing at one of the desks, talking in low voices. Were they talking about her? Did they know?

Then she saw who was standing among them. He was telling them some kind of story and his arms were waving around just like he did when he was excited.

A little shiver ran down her spine. She knew. She knew what he did when he was excited. Was that a good shiver or a bad shiver?

He leaned back and laughed and caught her eye. No. *That* was a shiver. One that sent electric pulses around her body.

She fixed her eyes on the floor and kept walking towards the treatment room. Her cheeks were warm and she wasn't normally the kind of girl who blushed. She wasn't normally the type of girl to lose sleep after a few kisses. Her lips had tingled for most of the night and when she'd taken her jacket off she'd caught a whiff of his aftershave. Just how close had they got?

She'd pulled back, laughing again, after the second kiss. Her stomach was doing backward flips and, with a mixture of alarm bells going off in her head and imaginary white unicorns charging around before her eyes, she wasn't quite sure what to think.

He'd looked thoughtful when she'd stepped back and hadn't pressed things any further. He'd slipped his hand into hers and they'd taken the subway back to the base.

Her skin had trembled as he'd walked her to the door of her house. She had felt like a teenager again, waiting for Don to throw the front door open and demand an introduction. But Avery was much cooler than she'd expected, he'd squeezed her hand and dropped a kiss on her head before walking away.

Don had been engrossed in his computer but had stood up when she'd appeared. 'Coffee?' he asked as he walked to the kitchen. 'I think I've missed dinner.'

No explanations were asked for. She was an adult. He didn't generally ask for a list of her activities. But once he realised she might be seeing a colleague she was quite sure Avery's file would fall across his desk.

Lily, one of the other nurses, looked up as she walked in. 'Katsuko—great. Can you check some diamorph with me? I've got a patient with a fractured femur and the Entonox gas is wearing off fast.'

Katsuko nodded, pleased to have something—anything—to do that would distract her. Checking controlled medicines was an everyday part of the job. She counted the vials, drew up the prescribed amount and locked up the cupboard. The patient in cubicle three was wincing as he moved. They double-checked his name and date of birth before administering the injection. 'Who are you on shift with today?' asked Lily.

Katsuko shook her head. 'Not sure. Haven't had the handover yet.'

They rounded the corner. Lily beamed. 'Oh, lucky you. It's our very own superhero, Avery. I kind of like him. He's fitting in well.'

The words were easy for Lily and she threw them out without a second thought. She was happily married, with her first baby on the way, and was currently seeing the world through a pink or blue hazy glow.

She'd been put onto night shift for the last part of her pregnancy as she hadn't been sleeping well and the night shifts were generally a little quieter.

Katsuko kept her gaze somewhere else. 'Yeah, he seems fine.'

Lily gave her a nudge. 'More than fine.'

'What's that supposed to mean?' It must have come out sharper than she'd meant because Lily looked surprised.

'Nothing.' She picked up her bag and stretched her back. 'Time for me to go. Keep an eye on my patient, will you? They'll be here to collect him soon for Theatre.'

Katsuko nodded and headed over to the desk for the handover report. It was swift. Twelve patients in the department. One for theatre, three kids with minor ailments, four elderly patients with a variety of chest conditions, one guy with an anaphylactic reaction to something and three other adults with minor ailments. The staff shared the patients out between them and got to work.

She was trying her absolute best to be cool. She was always calm and collected at work—nothing usually fazed her. So why did she feel like a bumbling wreck?

She messed up a sterile trolley while doing a simple dressing, then tripped over her own feet while walking to the treatment room.

The whole time she was working she was constantly looking over her shoulder, wondering where Avery was, and if anyone would notice something between them.

It was a couple of hours before he finally spoke to her. 'Katsuko, there's an ambulance bringing in one of the servicemen's teenagers. Can you give me a hand?'

Her response was automatic. She walked over to the sink

to wash her hands. Avery walked up behind her, his hand brushing against her bum.

'Don't!' she snapped.

They were at work. She was a professional. She wasn't the kind of girl to be caught in a compromising position in the treatment room or in the store.

At least that was the excuse she was letting bump around in her head.

It was nothing to do with the fact his kiss had driven her crazy. It was nothing to do with the things she'd shared with him—things she would never normally tell people. She'd worked with some of the people here for years and had never really shared about her grandmother. She could almost feel herself retreating a little. Trying to take back some of what she'd said.

Avery raised his eyebrows at her but didn't say a single word. He gave her a little hip-bump and washed his hands at the sink too. Katsuko grabbed an apron and some gloves and walked out to the receiving door. 'Do you know what's wrong?'

He frowned. 'Not clear. No accident. Sleepy and agitated.'

Katsuko joined in his frown. It wasn't exactly anything to go on. 'Age?' she asked. It could be anything. Alcohol, drugs, infection—the list was endless.

The ambulance appeared in the distance with the siren blaring. 'Nineteen.'

As it pulled up, Avery moved quickly to open the doors and pull the trolley towards him. The wheels automatically snapped down and allowed them to pull the trolley straight inside. The ambulance technician was talking rapidly in Japanese.

Katsuko walked alongside, translating as best she could. 'This is Jay Lim. He's nineteen. Came home last night and told his mother he wasn't feeling too well and went to bed.

When she tried to wake him for breakfast this morning she realised something was wrong and called an ambulance.'

'Let's take him into Resus.'

She wasn't surprised at those words. Although the report seemed bland—the condition of the patient wasn't. The technician shot out another round of words.

'Respirations high, forty, heart rate one-forty, and blood pressure one hundred over fifty-five. He's been aggressive and extremely tired. They haven't understood all of what he's saying.'

As soon as they hit the resus room Katsuko started hooking up the monitors for Jay. She turned to the technician and asked a quick question.

Her eyes met Avery's as she glanced at the oxygen saturation. 'No history of asthma so we can put him on oxygen.'

Frank Kelly hurried into the room. 'What do you need?'

'I need bloods—lots of them—and set up an IV.'

Avery turned back to Katsuko. 'Can they give us anything else?'

She looked over at the technician, asking swiftly in Japanese. A few seconds later she turned back to Avery. 'He's a keen windsurfer and was away for the last two nights at a competition.'

'Any chance he used drugs or alcohol?'

'The technician said they've had no report of that.'

He was the ultimate professional. She was starting to cringe at snapping at him a few minutes ago. A quiet word was all it would have taken. It was hard enough to fit in. The last thing she wanted was to give her colleagues anything to talk about.

Avery moved around the teenager quickly, pulling out his stethoscope and listening to his chest. He lifted his hand. 'Ask the technician to hang around for another few minutes.'

He carefully examined Jay's head and checked his pupils as Jay tried to bat him away. Then he checked his ears, which nearly earned him a punch.

'No chance he could have an undiagnosed head injury from the surfing?'

She asked again. 'Nothing reported.'

This was baffling her just as much as Avery.

He looked up. 'What's his temperature?'

She lifted a tympanic thermometer as she asked the technician. It was unusual he hadn't mentioned it in the handover. The technician shook his head. 'They couldn't get near his ears to get a temperature. He does feel warm to touch.'

Avery nodded to the technician to come back over and help hold Jay. 'Jay, we're just checking your temperature. Can you tell me how you're feeling?'

Katsuko was quick. The tympanic thermometer only took five seconds to register. Thank goodness. Because by six seconds, Jay was thrashing around again. He made a loud noise and then retched. Katsuko grabbed a nearby sick bowl, but it seemed that Jay didn't have much to bring up.

'Thirty-nine point five,' she said swiftly to Avery.

She could almost see his brain calculating everything. He watched as Frank nodded to another colleague who held Jay's arm firmly in place. Frank inserted a cannula and withdrew blood quickly, filling five different tubes.

Jay started to try and thrash again. 'It'll be enough,' said Avery. He walked over to the medicine cupboard in Resus. 'With a temperature like that there's likely to be an infection somewhere. His chest sounds clear, but call for an X-ray. The agitation is the thing that's worrying me most.'

Katsuko was watching him closely. Jay had been in the room around two minutes and she could already tell Avery was close to making a decision. At work he was decisive and trusted his instincts. She was learning to trust them too.

He caught her gaze. 'Can you ask the technician what the sleeping arrangements were for the surfing competition?'

She frowned. It was an odd question, but easily asked. She listened to the technician and turned back. 'It was university-style dorms.'

Avery nodded. 'I'm going down the meningitis route. There's no visible rash but we all know that seeing the rash is bad news. In an ideal world we'd do a lumbar puncture and get some CSF. But he's just too agitated right now. I'm going to have to make an executive decision. Let's start with some IV penicillin.' He looked around the room. 'Is there a relative? Can we ask about allergies?'

Katsuko held up the technician's paperwork. 'Mum was following the ambulance in the car. She told the technician Jay had no allergies. Do you want me to find her and double-check?'

Avery shook his head. 'If it's already recorded that's good enough for me. Let's not waste another second for this kid.' He mixed up the preparation and drew it up into a syringe. 'Frank, can you hold his arm while I administer this?'

Frank nodded and held Jay's arm firmly. Avery slotted the syringe into the cannula. IV antibiotics had to be administered over a few minutes and Avery watched the clock while he completed the process.

He met her gaze again. 'I'll talk to his mother as soon as she arrives. Jay needs one-to-one nursing care. Fifteen-minute obs. IV fluids. I'd love to monitor fluid intake and output but I'm not sure that inserting a catheter is feasible right now. I want his breathing watched carefully and also his oxygen saturation. I'll write up some other meds for temperature control, nausea and agitation if required, along with the rest of his IV antibiotics. We need to watch this boy carefully.' He gave a little shake of his head. 'I'd still prefer to have got some CSF.'

She could see the worry lines on his forehead. Meningitis could be a killer. If this was the correct diagnosis they had to hope they'd administered antibiotics quickly enough to have an impact and halt the progression of the disease. Frank disappeared with the blood bottles and forms and she walked over next to Avery. She knew that testing cerebrospinal fluid could be a crucial part of the diagnosis. But the procedure for a lumbar puncture meant the patient had to lie very still in a certain position. Jay just wasn't able to do that right now.

'You okay?'

She watched as he licked his lips and took a few seconds to answer. He looked up. All she could see was the pale green of his eyes. She was closer than she meant to be. But it was natural for her. The skin on their arms was touching and it felt like that was meant to happen.

It was the first time she'd actually seen Avery look a little vulnerable. Something inside her squeezed tight. She reached up and touched the side of his face. 'You've got this, Avery.'

Her voice was low and his head inched a little closer to hers. Their noses almost touched. 'Do you need to tell me something?'

He shook his head. 'I'm just not good with waiting games. I want to know right now if meningitis is the correct diagnosis. The penicillin won't do any harm. But I want to know right now if it's doing any good.'

She gave a little smile. 'Avery Flynn, do you have no patience?'

He smiled too. 'Not a single bit.'

She licked her lips. 'Then let's get logical.' She tilted her head to one side. 'Tell me why meningitis.'

Avery nodded. 'Teenage boy, quick onset, he's probably immunised against some strains of meningitis but not every type. Neisseria meningitis is most common in teenagers, particularly if they've been in a communal environment. It could be serotype C, Y or W.'

She put her hand on his arm. 'And you could have just saved his life.'

It was the oddest feeling. But since her palm was in contact with his warm skin she didn't feel the urge at all to pull it away. It was pathetic. Look at how she'd acted when he'd brushed against her behind. Why did this feel like exactly what she should be doing?

Avery glanced over at Jay. 'Let's hope so. The next few hours will be crucial.' He straightened up. 'Is his mother here yet? I'll need to speak to her.'

Katsuko pulled back her hand. 'I'll go and check.' She stepped back and hurried down the corridor.

Avery stared at his arm for a few seconds. He could almost feel her imprinted on his skin. There was a distinct feeling of unease. It had only been a few short days but he'd made a real connection with Katsuko and he wasn't quite sure what to do next.

The initial harmless flirting had quickly turned into something else. Every relationship he'd ever been involved in had been cool on his part. He'd been happy for the companionship. Enjoyed the friendships and physical connection. But the emotional connection? On his part, it had never really been there.

But Katsuko felt different. He wanted to be around her. He wanted to know so much about her. It would be easier if she weren't the General's daughter. It would be *so* much easier if she weren't the Major General's daughter.

But no matter how much he was feeling the first real pull at his heartstrings, the little twist inside was still there. Japan? He hardly knew anything about it. He wasn't even entirely sure how long this assignment would last. Apparently his sick colleague had requested this posting to Okatu.

It was likely that once he'd made a full recovery he'd want to pick this assignment up again.

Part of those thoughts felt like relief. He wouldn't want to settle down. He wouldn't want to put down roots anywhere. He wouldn't be in the difficult position of having that kind of a conversation with a woman because he always had a get-out clause.

It didn't matter that he'd known lots of fellow colleagues who had found love, married and happily combined their family lives with working in the air force. Sure, it was difficult. Sure, there were sacrifices to make.

The whole thing had just never computed for him because of his example of family life back home. He'd loved the freedom of the air force. It gave him a safe haven. It had become his family. Could he even contemplate something else?

A dark hand appeared on his arm. Frank. 'Avery? Jay's mother has arrived. I've put her in the relatives' room. Katsuko is with her.'

'Thanks very much. You'll keep an eye on him while I'm gone?'

Frank gave him a resolute nod.

The relatives' room was bland. It didn't matter how hard the staff tried to make it warm and friendly, it was always a place where difficult news was delivered, and it seemed to have that atmosphere around it permanently.

As soon as he walked in, Jay's mother jumped to her feet. 'Where is he? Where is Jay? Why can't I see him?'

Katsuko had her lips pressed together and Avery could sense the tension in her body.

He reached out and touched the woman. She had the broadest Texan accent he'd ever heard. It was such a surprise. In the last few days he'd become accustomed to the quieter tones of Japanese voices or Japanese accents when colleagues were speaking in English to him.

'You can see Jay, but I need to make a few things clear.' He spoke calmly and honestly. 'Where is Jay's dad?'

The colour faded from the woman's face. 'Why?'

Avery shook his head. 'Jay's sick. I think he might have meningitis. The next few hours are crucial. It would be best if his dad could be here too.'

Jay's mum took a little step backwards. 'He's…a pilot. He's flying to Kadena Air Base, then onto Okinawa. He won't be home until tomorrow.'

Katsuko looked at him. 'Do you want me to deal with that?'

Avery nodded. He didn't know what she'd do—he was just sure that as the General's daughter she could sort whatever she needed to.

She turned to Jay's mother. 'Can you give me your husband's name and rank?'

'Captain Rizalino Lim.'

Something flashed across Katsuko's face for the briefest of seconds before she disappeared out of the door.

Avery wasn't sure but the name sounded Filipino. The mother was distinctly American. A huge percentage of US Air Force families were from different nationalities. Had Katsuko just had a flash of familiarity with this family?

The call to her father took moments. His secretary answered straight away. 'It's Katsuko. There's a medical issue. A parent is required to be located. We have a teenager with a suspected diagnosis of meningitis. He's being treated but the next few hours are crucial.'

'Details?'

'Pilot. Captain Rizalino Lim. He's flying to Kadena, then Okinawa today.'

'I'll find the details while I put you through to the General.'

Katsuko could almost hear her fingers fly across the keyboard. Her father had always been great when families had medical emergencies on the base. He would do everything he could to find the relative and get them back to their family. On occasion, it couldn't happen. But nine times out of ten her father would make sure it did.

'Something wrong?'

She smiled. He was all business. She quickly explained. If she closed her eyes for a second she could picture him. With one hand he'd be playing with a pencil, making little notes on the pad in front of him. He'd be nodding his head slowly too.

There was a loud creaking noise. His door.

'Ah, that's Leah with the details. Give me a second. Hmm...yes. Yes, that should be fine. Katsuko, tell Mrs Lim that arrangements are being made for her husband to be with her and Jay as soon as possible. Leah will also arrange for one of our welfare officers to come and wait with her until her husband arrives. Everything else okay?'

She was surprised. When she phoned him about air force business he didn't tend to talk about anything else. 'Yes, why shouldn't it be?'

'I haven't seen much of you these last few days.'

Her skin prickled a little. 'Don, I'm twenty-five. I have a social life.'

'Any kind of social life I should know about?'

Now her whole body prickled. Someone had told him—told him that she was spending time with Avery. There was nothing surer.

She looked instantly over her shoulder. If her father knew, there was no point pretending her colleagues hadn't noticed things too. She might as well have a neon sign flashing above her head.

She gave a silent shake of her head. Don would soon get around to asking her outright. She'd just need to figure out what kind of answer she was going to give him.

'Nothing you should know, Don. Don't worry.'

She put down the phone and sucked in a deep breath. Her head didn't know what to do with this information. She spun around and saw Avery's outline behind the darkened window of the relatives' room.

Darn it. She even liked his reflection. And as for the unexpected feel and taste of his lips on hers the other night… She squeezed her eyes shut. Thinking about it pushed every other thought from her brain. Not something she could do at work—ever.

She straightened her shoulders and walked back down the corridor, entering the relatives' room and giving Mrs Lim a reassuring smile. 'General Williams wants to assure you he's making arrangements to get your husband back to be with you both.' She held out her hand. 'Will we take Mrs Lim along to sit with her son?'

He put a gentle arm around Mrs Lim and led her down towards the resus room. Mrs Lim put her hand up to her mouth when she saw Jay. Frank came over to join her and waited patiently while Avery explained what he could. 'At this point we have to look at why Jay's having these symptoms. Meningitis is a likely cause and it's something that has to be treated straight away. Because of that we've got Jay on some intravenous antibiotics. We also have him on some other drugs for some of the other symptoms he's having. He's agitated, has been vomiting and has a high temperature. We need to monitor Jay very carefully for the next few hours. You're welcome to stay and sit with him.'

She turned around. 'But he's had injections for meningitis. It can't be that.'

Avery nodded and pointed towards the computer. 'We're lucky. I have access to Jay's medical records. He has had some vaccinations for Hib, a strain of meningitis, and Men C, another strain. But there are many different types of meningitis and we don't have vaccines for them all.'

'So this is a different kind?'

Avery nodded. 'We think so. We've taken some blood from him for testing—the results will show if there are bacteria in his blood. Unfortunately, the other test we need to do is called a lumbar puncture. We'd have to curl Jay on his side and put a needle into a specific part of his spine to collect some fluid. Jay is just too agitated to do that test.'

'Will it matter?' Her eyes were wide.

He took a deep breath. 'We might not be able to specify the exact type of meningitis, but we would still be able to identify it as a bacterial meningitis.'

'Would his treatment change?'

Avery shook his head. 'It would still be intravenous antibiotics. We just need to wait and see how he is over the next few hours.'

Frank came over to show Mrs Lim to a seat. He gave a nod to Avery and Katsuko. 'I'll give you a shout if I need you.'

Katsuko gave Avery a little smile. Both of them could recognise the signs of being told unofficially to take a break. They were lucky. The ER had its own coffee room. Staff here frequently didn't have time to make it to the hospital canteen or other facilities.

Katsuko flicked the switch on the kettle and opened the huge tin that sat in the middle of the coffee table.

Avery looked over her shoulder and pulled something out. 'What are these things? I see them everywhere.'

She gave a laugh as she spooned some coffee into the mugs. 'I think you'd call them…' she pointed to the first packet '…chocolate pretzel sticks, and those ones…' she pointed to the other '…are strawberry rice cakes.'

Avery was still staring at the pictures on the packaging.

She poured some water into the cups. 'They are two of most popular snacks in Japan. Think of it as an initiation of fire.'

He pulled open the first packet and sagged down onto a chair as Katsuko tipped some milk into the mugs, stirred the coffee and brought them over. She hesitated for a second, then sat down next to him. There wasn't much point in worrying if someone saw them sitting together.

Avery settled back, letting his shoulder come into contact with hers. 'Okay, introduce me to your strange snacks. I wanted potato chips and a candy bar.'

She raised her eyebrows. 'What? No apples or bananas?'

'Usually yes. But today? After that diagnosis? Definitely something sweet and nasty.'

She handed him the chocolate pretzel sticks. He took a few and started eating. After a few minutes he smiled, picking up his coffee and relaxing a little. 'Hey, these are actually okay. I could get used to these.'

'You'll have to. There isn't much else in the tin.'

He turned his head towards her. 'So, you're off in a few days. Where are we going?'

She was trying so hard to appear like the coolest woman on the planet as she felt all the blood starting to rush to her cheeks and ruin her disguise.

And, for some strange reason, *What makes you think we're going anywhere?* turned into, 'Where do you want to go?' She wasn't entirely sure how that had happened.

What had happened to the walls she'd wanted to build around herself earlier? The fact she didn't really want to give her colleagues anything to talk about? It seemed a few hours in the company of Avery Flynn made her go against all the things she'd planned in her head.

He gave a little nod. 'You took me to the busiest place on the planet the last time. This time I'd like to go somewhere a little quieter.'

Uh-oh. Those pale green eyes were staring at her. And there was a definite twinkle in them. She didn't want her brain to start imagining what he was hinting at. If that was what he'd done in the busiest place on the planet, what could he do somewhere quieter?

She gave a little nod. 'Tokyo is huge. I'm sure I can find us somewhere more scenic to go.'

He grinned. 'And definitely quieter?'

There he went again, teasing her. She could play him at his own game.

'I have the perfect place in mind.'

CHAPTER SIX

HE'D TOLD KATSUKO he would pick her up at home but she'd suggested they meet in the base coffee shop. Part of him was relieved and part of him was a little put out. Was she trying to hide him from her father? And did he really want to be under the General's interrogating gaze anyway?

He blinked as she walked in. Katsuko was wearing a bright red dress patterned with dark flowers. He'd never seen her in a dress before—he'd never even seen her in a casual skirt before and he was surprised by how much it suited her. The dress was decorated with black flowers that matched her sharp dark hair.

She had a red leather bag slung across her body, black shoes with a cork sole and bright red lipstick.

She shot him a smile and joined him in the queue. 'What are you having?'

You. On this base that response would probably get him jail time.

'Just a cappuccino. You're looking gorgeous. I feel distinctly underdressed.' He tugged at his polo shirt.

She waved her hand with a smile that made him curious. 'You don't need to worry.' She nodded to the cashier. 'I'll have a skinny latte to go.' While they waited for their drinks he tried to tease out of her what their plans were for the day.

'I heard Jay is out of ICU and on the road to recovery.'

'Yeah, I went up to see him last night. He was tetchy. I think people forget that even though antibiotics fight off meningitis, the recovery process can be slow. At least he's a teenager. He can tell us how he feels. Think of all the poor babies and toddlers who can't put into words how they feel for the next few months.'

He'd noticed something else. The whole time he'd been around Jay's mother she'd seemed quite rigid. But as soon as her husband had appeared she'd just crumpled. It was like she had been holding herself together until he'd been there to catch her. Their devotion to each other and their son had shone through. Their relief at having each other there had been almost palpable. It was a connection that he'd never seen between his parents—or their future partners. Another reminder of how little his family actually functioned.

She was looking at him a little strangely. 'What?'

She shrugged. 'You're quite sentimental. I didn't take you for that.'

He gave her a crafty look. 'I have lots of hidden qualities. You just have to find them.' He waved his hand. 'Anyway, you didn't tell me what to bring. Should I change?'

This time she laughed. 'Believe me, you don't need to change. You'll be fine just as you are.' She leaned forward to pick up their coffees. 'At least I think you are.'

'What does that mean?'

She shot him a cheeky wink. 'All will be revealed. Let's go.'

They headed to the subway and Katsuko bought them tickets to a station he'd never heard of. The gleam in her eye was unmistakeable.

It felt like payback. He'd hinted at something the other day. And he was still waiting for a response. She was hard to read. At work, it seemed like she only focused on the job.

That was good. But it meant that there was only the occasional glimpse of what lay beneath the surface. She hadn't objected when he'd suggested they see each other again. In fact, she'd responded almost immediately. But what was normal for Katsuko? He had no idea.

The subway wasn't quite as busy as it had been the last time and he sat down next to her. 'Tell me about your assignments.'

'Why do you want to know about them?'

She shrugged. 'Because you've been on lots of overseas assignments. I've only ever gone to Georgia to complete my nurse training.'

'I spent some time in Georgia. It's a pity we missed each other.' Did she even realise how gorgeous she looked today?

'Where else have you been?'

He settled back into the seat. 'Ohio, Florida, Arizona, Texas, Afghanistan, Germany and Italy.'

'What was your favourite?'

'They all had something good. I probably learned the most in Afghanistan. It's a combat zone—nothing else compares to that. You never know what is going to happen next. Florida had fantastic surf and weather. Texas was good for me as doctor. I got to shadow one of the doctors at NASA for a few weeks and learn a little about the qualifications I'd need to go into that field.'

Her smile was broad. 'That sounds fabulous. Will you do it?'

'I might. Competition is tough. I'd need to go back to Dayton, Ohio, and study aerospace medicine for a couple of years.' He gave her a nudge. 'Fancy being a nurse out there?'

She gave a little sigh and stared off into space. 'A world of possibilities. I'm just not sure. I love being in Japan, but I'm a member of the US Air Force. I think it might be good for me to try someplace else.'

'Because of your grandmother?'

'Yes. And no. I'd hate to leave and something happen to her. I'm all the family she's got left—even if she doesn't want me. But sometimes I wonder just how long I should wait.'

'What does the General say?'

She bit her lip. It took her a few moments to answer. 'We don't really talk about it much. Apparently he was a bit of a bear for the few months I was away in Georgia—even though he's never said anything about it to me. We've never really discussed the fact that I should probably be based somewhere else. A few other colleagues have been and gone in the space of time that I've been here.' She rubbed her hands on her thighs. 'I kind of wonder if he feels like me?'

'What do you mean?'

'He's practically put his life on hold to raise me. Don's a good-looking guy. And he's fun. I'm quite sure there are a whole host of women out there that he could have made a connection with and didn't.'

It was instant. He could tell there was something else. 'So why didn't he?'

She shook her head and lowered her gaze, so he reached over and put his hand on hers. 'Why do *you* think he didn't?'

'Sometimes I wonder if he was a little in love with my mother. He's never said anything that led me to believe that, but he talks about her with real respect and affection.'

'And how does he talk about your dad?'

She gave a little smile. 'Much the same.' The subway trundled to a stop and she looked up. 'It's the next station.' Her fingers reached up and twiddled with her hair. 'Then maybe the women that he's met didn't want to be lumbered with someone else's child.'

Avery shook his head. 'Please tell me you don't actually think that?'

Her brown eyes met his. 'Why not? There are lots of

women in this life who wouldn't want to take on someone else's child. What if the love of Don's life came along and he let her slip through his fingers because of me?' There was a little wobble in her voice. He was struggling with this—probably because he could see her emotions bubbling underneath the surface.

'You're an adult, Katsuko. Not a child. Let me put it this way. Do you honestly think Don would have a serious relationship with the kind of woman who would make him choose between you and her? He doesn't strike me as that kind of guy.'

She gave a sad kind of smile. 'Probably not. I just hate to think that I'm the reason he's stayed all these years and now I'm thinking about leaving.'

He grabbed her hand as the subway pulled into the next station. 'All kids grow up and leave home. You've just left it a little later than normal.'

They exited the subway and she led him up a flight of steps. This part of Tokyo wasn't quite as built up. It was lighter, with areas of green around them. The station was part way up a mountain that gave a good view over the city.

'Where on earth are we?'

'It's all part of my master plan. Have you heard of a *sento*?'

'A what?'

She held out her hands. 'They're all around here. A *sento* is a bathhouse.'

He looked stunned. 'A bathhouse?'

'Yes. The other alternative is an *onsen*, which is built around a hot spring. There is a whole variety around here. Some are completely modern, some more traditionally built.'

She could see him look around the area. Some of the buildings were sleek, rising out of the mountainside and sheeted in glass. Others were constructed from wood, painted white, with their large, dark, gently curved roofs being the most visually impressive component. She pointed to the one straight in front of them. 'This one is my favourite. It's a super-*sento*.'

Avery stopped walking. 'So, what actually happens in a super-*sento*?'

She was trying very hard not to grin. Avery had hinted about getting her alone. He had no idea what he was about to get into.

She smiled sweetly. 'It's a traditional bathhouse.' She gave him a wink. 'And it's communal.' She walked swiftly ahead.

'What?' Avery's voice shouted after her. Then his footsteps pounded along and he pulled at her shoulder. 'What did you just say?'

She'd reached the door of the *sento* and pulled it open. 'Bathhouses in Japan are communal.'

He paused at the door, his mouth hanging open. 'But I didn't bring my swimmers.'

'Who says you need swimmers?' She couldn't help but laugh—he looked rooted to the spot. She pulled out her bag and paid at Reception. It only took a few seconds for Avery to appear at her shoulder.

From the expression on his face he'd collected his thoughts in a whole different direction. His smile reached from one side of his face to the other. Everything was going perfectly to plan.

She pointed off to the right and handed him a key. 'You go that way—I go to the left. Take off your clothes in the changing room. There will be pyjamas or a loose kimono inside for you to change into. Leave all your other things in the locker, then head inside.'

He was still smiling. 'I'll see you inside, then.' He walked towards the door—no, he swaggered towards the door and Katsuko almost burst out laughing.

The receptionist was smiling at her broadly. She'd seen it all before.

The next hour or so would be interesting.

Avery just about flung his clothes into the locker and pulled on the pyjamas. They were thin and light—almost like a pair of surgical scrubs. He moved outside and looked up. It was a bright corridor, sealed off from the outside world but clearly outdoors. Ahead was another door.

He couldn't stop smiling. He pushed the door open and stopped walking promptly.

The room was filled with naked men and steam. Lots of steam. An assistant gestured for him to take off his clothes. He paused, he couldn't help it. Avery had never been embarrassed by his body and it was apparent that every single man in this room felt the same way. He was a doctor—there was nothing he hadn't seen before. Men of all shapes and sizes stood in front of him. Most of them were chatting to each other as if they were fully clothed. Nakedness didn't seem to be an issue.

Avery pulled off his pyjamas and sat on the stool that the smiling assistant pointed to—it was obvious he was used to visitors. Two seconds later he was hit by a warm shower spray and handed what looked like a kind of loofah.

He gave a nod and scrubbed at his skin while the warm shower buzzed over him. When he was finished the assistant gestured for him to walk further on. Ahead, was the biggest array of large tubs he'd ever seen. Some were empty, some had a few men in them, and others were busy. To the side were rooms with a range of glass doors that looked like saunas.

He stuck his toe in the nearest tub and pulled it out sharply. The water was near scalding. The doctor in him wanted to tell everyone not to go near it. But a few seconds later a man who resembled a sumo wrestler stepped into the tub with no trepidation whatsoever.

For a minute Avery forgot all about his nakedness. Any second now the guy would have a heart attack in water at that temperature. Instead, the man spread his arms out around the side of the tub and leaned back, as if it was his favourite place in the world.

Avery gave his head a little shake and moved forward. He dipped his toe in a variety of tubs. They ranged from scalding to very hot to hot. The next tub had only one man in it and the water temperature was warm and pleasant. The man gave him a gracious nod that made Avery feel it was impossible to walk away.

He gave a nod too and climbed in. The water was soothing. It instantly relaxed his tense muscles. He kept glancing around. First of all, at the other tub where he kept expecting the large man to faint, then around the whole bathing area.

It took him a few seconds to realise that Katsuko was nowhere in sight. In fact, no women were anywhere in sight.

The man in his tub nodded towards him again. 'Visitor?'

Avery smiled. He really did need to learn some Japanese. 'Yes.'

The man smiled politely. 'Okatu base?'

Avery laughed and nodded. He might as well have a sign on his forehead that said he was American.

'Pilot?'

He shook his head. 'No, doctor.'

'Ah. Doctor. Good.' He gave him a thoughtful glance and pointed to the tub. 'First time?'

Yes, it seemed he did have a sign on his head.

'It is, yes.'

The man pointed further down the bathhouse. 'Try bath with tea.'

'Tea?'

He gave a knowing nod. 'Yes.'

Avery was surprised. He'd never heard of a bath with tea. When Katsuko had told him not to bring anything she hadn't been joking. Towels were everywhere. Along with soap, shampoo, moisturising lotion and cotton swabs. But no one actually used these products in the water. They only used them in the showers.

He rested his head back for a moment and closed his eyes. Katsuko had surprised him. When she'd brought him into a bathhouse and hinted they'd be naked his mind had naturally gone into overdrive—just as she'd intended.

He almost laughed out loud. She'd got him. Fair and square. She'd led him right up the proverbial path.

He couldn't wipe away the grin as he opened his eyes again and stared around the vast bathhouse at the wide variety of naked men. Of all the places in the world to come…

He nodded to the other man and climbed back out, walking along—not particularly conscious of his nakedness—past the variety of other tubs. Some were bubbling with jets. One definitely looked like green tea. Another had a very odd aroma. No one was in it and he bent down to have a closer smell. He almost spluttered. Red wine? In a bathhouse?

He looked around to see if anyone was watching. Everyone was going about their daily business, so he dipped his finger into the water and brought it up to his nose. Definitely red wine. He'd seen everything now.

He had a half a mind to climb into it. Cleopatra had apparently bathed in red wine. If it was good enough for the Egyptians…

Five seconds later he was in the wine.

It was the oddest feeling. The smell was so strong and the feeling exuberant. And it was hot. Very hot. Was it possible to boil in a tub of wine? He'd never seen this much wine before and he was pretty sure people could get drunk on the fumes alone.

A few minutes was long enough, then he headed back to the showers and tried to scrub the smell of wine from his skin. He could just imagine the look on Blake Anderson's face tomorrow morning if he turned up smelling of wine.

Curiosity was killing him. There had to be a women-only section in here too. He could only imagine it was completely hidden from view, otherwise it would be every teenage boy's dream.

As he headed to the changing room he was surprised by the time. He'd been in here for more than an hour and a half. One of the assistants signalled for him to put back on the scrubs-like pyjamas and head through another door.

He should have guessed. Katsuko had the widest grin he'd ever seen and was sprawled across a chaise longue.

'How do you like a Japanese bathhouse?' she teased.

He pushed her legs over and sat down beside her. 'I can think of a few improvements.'

'I wonder what they might be. Did you enjoy the experience?'

He raised his eyebrows. 'What's not to enjoy? If I didn't know enough about body shapes before, I certainly do now. Once I got over the shock of being naked among complete strangers I was kind of hoping there might have been naked females around too.'

'I bet you were.' She shook her head. 'But the bathing is always completely separate. Some super-*sento*s are more equipped for families. They have mixed bathing and everyone wears swimsuits. But I thought I should show you the genuine Japanese experience.' She looked around. 'It's usually busier when I come. Most people come to the bathhouses in the evening rather than during the day. I just wanted to give you a gentle introduction.'

'You think I needed it?'

She swung her legs to the floor. 'What do you want to do next? There's a bar upstairs and there's a restaurant. There are also some rooftop footbaths or there's a low-temperature sauna—you keep your clothes on in there.'

A few teenage girls walked past, their wet hair tied up in ponytails. They were looking at him and Katsuko and whispering together.

He shifted in the chair. They must have been in the bathhouse at the same time as Katsuko. It was clear she'd noticed their actions. She waved her hand. 'Pay no notice, they're just silly schoolgirls. One of them was talking about me while she was sitting next to me. She nearly died when I turned around and answered her in perfect Japanese.' She raised her eyebrows. 'I even corrected her grammar for her.'

Was this the kind of thing Katsuko experienced regularly? He tried to temper the little flame burning inside him. He glared at the teenagers. 'Silly schoolgirls who should know better,' he said.

He turned back towards her. It was clear that Katsuko didn't want to take this any further. He could see her biting her lip.

He shook his head and bent down. 'What's wrong? You're better than this. You're stronger than this.'

She closed her eyes for the briefest of seconds. When she opened them again he saw a whole host of vulnerability in the tiniest of flashes. 'Welcome to my life, Avery. Just as well you don't plan on being around too long. You'd have to get used to it, just like I have.' Her voice was barely a whisper. The most fleeting of glances was taking the whole shine off their day.

He didn't know where the words came from. They were just on his lips and out there before his brain had processed them. 'And I would. Every. Single. Day.'

Both of them froze. He hadn't meant to say them. Of course he would be leaving soon. He didn't even know what *this* was.

Those deep brown eyes of hers were like a bottomless

pool. They'd sparkled earlier. He liked them best like that. He wanted to bring that back. That was all this really was. That was all this could ever really be.

Her eyes blinked shut again for a second. *He knew.*

He knew she wasn't really taking him seriously.

But when she opened them again it was as if she were giving herself a mental shake. She was putting it all behind her.

Part of his heart twanged as her mask slipped back into place and she smiled up at him.

He took a deep breath. It was time to get things back on track. 'What do you have in store for me this afternoon?'

She stood up, arching her back and stretching. His eyes were instantly drawn to one place. Underwear didn't appear to be required under the pyjamas. Any more thoughts like that and he'd need to find his jeans again.

She put her hands on her hips and looked at him. 'Today is all about culture. I'm introducing you to some of the most famous Japanese pastimes.'

'Do any of these pastimes involve food?'

She laughed. 'You should know me by now. They all involve food. We've got a bit of a journey next. Why don't we grab a drink and something to eat before we head out?'

She headed for the stairs and he followed close behind. He'd just spent ninety minutes in one of the hottest places he'd ever been, yet Katsuko still looked immaculate.

'Did you even go into the bathhouse? How come your hair hasn't frizzed in the steam? You don't have a hair out of place.'

She turned in the stairwell and put a hand on his shoulder. Because of their position on the stairs her breasts were directly in his line of vision. Some things just couldn't be complained about.

'I told you. I've been coming here for years. It only takes

me five minutes to fix my hair as they have hairdryers and straighteners in the changing room.'

'You straighten your hair?'

She gave him an astonished look. '*Every* girl straightens her hair.'

He shrugged. 'Good to know. Must have missed that one.'

They walked into the bar and sat at one of the tables. Avery went to pick up the menu but she put her hand on his. 'Can I give you a recommendation?'

'If I let you, can I claim a reward?' The words came out instantly. He could feel the connection again. Feel the buzz between them. The truth was, it never seemed to go away. He couldn't remember ever feeling like this.

But he could remember someone talking about it. His father. He'd always talked about feeling electricity between him and whatever number wife he was on. The trouble was, the electricity always shorted out. His father lost interest quickly and moved on.

Katsuko leaned across the glass-topped table towards him. He couldn't imagine ever losing interest in her and he'd barely even scratched the surface. There was just that tiny little gnawing feeling that he didn't want to end up like his father.

'Has anyone ever told you that you can be quite cheeky?'

'Has anyone ever told you that you bring out the best and the worst in them?'

She sat back a little, the smile dropping from her face. 'I bring out the worst in you?'

His stomach churned. Wrong, wrong thing to say. He'd been thinking too much. Drawing comparisons with a man he'd never had anything in common with. He covered quickly, leaning across the table again and whispering, 'You bring out lots of bad thoughts in me.'

There was a second of silence, then she smiled again as

the waiter appeared. She spoke rapidly in Japanese to him and he nodded and disappeared.

'What did you order?'

'Two beers and two portions of prawn and pork pancake with caramelised onions and crispy noodles. Trust me, it's delicious.'

He groaned. 'I trust you already. It sounds delicious. How long will it take them to bring it out?'

'Ten minutes.' She tilted her head to one side. 'This is the first time I've seen you out of work without your hat.'

His hand went automatically to his head. 'I know. I had no idea where we might go. I know there are a lot of theme parks in Tokyo. I didn't want to lose my hat on the first ride.'

'You thought I might take you to a theme park?'

He held up one hand. 'I had no idea. I thought you might be a bit of an adrenaline junkie.'

She frowned. It was obviously an expression she wasn't familiar with.

He waved his hands. 'You know, someone who likes motor racing, bungee jumping and parachuting.'

She shuddered. She actually shuddered. 'Not a chance.'

He was amazed. 'But at work you seem fearless—you don't like theme parks?'

She counted off on her fingers. 'I don't like roller-coasters, I don't like things that make you go upside down, things that shoot you into the air. I definitely don't like ghost trains.' She held out her hand and gave it a little shake. 'I don't mind simulator rides because I know they're not real, and I *might* go on a water ride depending on how big the drop is.'

'You're really a big scaredy-cat. I'm so surprised.'

She shrugged as the waiter brought over their drinks. She took a sip from her beer bottle and gave him a wink. 'Maybe I just like to surprise you.'

Was she joking? Pulling his leg because she wasn't really scared of anything?

A gorgeous smell wafted towards them as the kitchen door swung open. He waited until the plates had been put down and the waiter had walked away. He picked up the chopsticks and wondered how on earth he could do this without getting into a mess.

Katsuko was staring at him as if she had something else on her mind. 'You already surprised me,' he said as he tried to grab some of the pork.

'I did?'

'You got me naked on our third date.'

This guy was going to drive her plain crazy. She hated to admit that she loved being in his company. But one minute he seemed to flirt like crazy and the next he seemed to back off. Yet if he did anything else as well as he kissed…

She had to keep reminding herself he'd been gentlemanly earlier. He hadn't really meant what he'd said. He had been protective of her. And that was nice. It was kind. But she had to remember it wasn't more than that.

She took him to the train station and listened to him talk about his favourite places in America for most of the journey. He was reluctant at first but she was glad that she'd asked. After a few questions his answers grew more passionate and she could see the love for the place reflected in his eyes. By the time they reached Komagome Station she knew that he loved the Lincoln Memorial, the Smithsonian and an original nineteen-fifties diner back in Ohio. The one thing she did notice was that his memories all seemed attached to his uncle—none of them were about his mother or father. It seemed odd. Her favourite places were always associated with the people she'd been there with, a few with her parents and a few with Don. None with her grandmother.

'Your family must miss you,' she said as they rode on the train.

He blinked. 'What do you mean?'

'You've been to lots of overseas bases. You've moved around a lot. Don't they get tired of it all and ask when you'll come home?'

It seemed a natural question. She knew it was one that Don would ask her if she moved base.

He hesitated. And in that second her insides curled up a little.

'My family aren't the most...traditional.'

'And mine is?'

She could see him thinking about what to say. He met her gaze. 'The picture you carry, of your mum and dad? I think it's safe to say my mum and dad have never looked at each other like that. They weren't a match made in heaven. In fact, both of them seem to have made it their life's ambition to get married as many times as possible. My sister seems to be learning from their examples.'

She was stunned. The way he'd delivered the words made it clear this topic wasn't really open for discussion. She licked her lips and said quietly, 'People can make mistakes.' They were pulling into the station.

Avery must have recognised the English signs as he stood up. 'But wouldn't it be nice if they learned from them?' he muttered.

They walked out of the train station into the clean, fresh air.

'Where are we?' Avery looked around.

She pointed forward. She'd just glimpsed a tiny part of the man that was Avery Flynn. She was curious to know more. But not curious enough to press where she shouldn't.

'This is Rikugien. It's my favourite Japanese garden in Tokyo. It is so peaceful you can easily forget that you are in the city.' She held out her arms as they walked towards the entrance. 'And we've come at the perfect time of year. It's gorgeous in autumn when the maple trees turn a stunning blend of red and yellow. The only time of year it looks better is spring when all the pink cherry blossom is out.'

She turned and he was watching her carefully. 'First a bathhouse and now a Japanese garden? You're like a different person today, much more chill.'

She stepped up right under his nose and whispered, 'Say the word, Avery, and I'll take you shopping. I can guarantee complete and utter chaos.'

He slid his hand into hers. 'I think I'll stick with the Japanese garden.'

They wandered around the gardens for nearly an hour. The main part of the gardens had a large central pond surrounded by hills and trees. Katsuko led him to a bridge and stopped halfway. 'Look over there. That's *garyu-seki*.'

He wrinkled his nose as he stared at the half-submerged rock in the water surrounded by a whole array of turtles. 'What does that mean?'

'It's called the sleeping dragon rock.' She gave him a nudge. 'If you close your eyes and squint a little it looks like a dragon.' She couldn't hide the hint of laughter in her voice.

He tilted his head from one side to the other, obviously trying to picture the rocks as a dragon. 'It might have helped if they'd painted it.'

She laughed. 'You're supposed to use your imagination.'

He pointed to the widely dispersed small buildings surrounding the pond. 'What are those?'

Something inside her fluttered. She'd had lots of different colleagues from all parts of the world. It wasn't the first time she'd taken someone sightseeing around Tokyo, but sightseeing with Avery felt different than normal.

No one else had kissed her at the Hachiko Crossing. Most people wanted to go to sumo wrestling or one of the theme parks. She'd never really shown a colleague the things that she loved in Tokyo. The things that she would miss most if she ever left.

She stepped a little closer. 'If I tell you, will you promise to behave?'

He put his hand on her hip, pulling her closer to him. 'Me? Behave? After you've already gotten me naked?'

She shook her head. He was going to bring this up for ever. A little breeze blew between them, sweeping her hair across her face. His fingers reached up and stroked her face, catching the hair and tucking it behind her ear.

For a second she was lost. It was like an instant flash forward to something that would never exist. She'd kind of like to feel like this for ever. She could picture him in fifty years' time, telling their family that Katsuko had got him naked on their third date.

She sucked in her breath sharply. Where had that come from?

'You okay?' He must have seen her moment of panic. His stubble brushed against her ear and she caught her breath again. Time to focus.

She nodded. 'Those are Japanese tea houses. I thought you might like to visit one and see a traditional Japanese tea ceremony.' She held up her hand. 'But be warned. It takes just under an hour. You'll have to learn some patience.'

He caught her unawares, leaning forward and brushing his lips against hers. 'You're teaching me everything I need to know about patience.'

If he hadn't stepped back when he did she would have responded instantly, wrapping her arms around his neck and demanding to be kissed like before. Instead, he slipped his hand into hers again and gave it a little tug.

She pointed to the nearest tea house. 'This is the one we'll go to. It's built from wood from the Meiji period. It survived the war.'

'What's the Meiji period?'

'It was the late eighteen hundreds right up until the First World War.'

The free-standing tea house had a good view of the sleeping dragon, built in an arbour on a stream that ran through a gorge. The water fell down through the rocks, sending a light spray into the air, and a large collection of koi circled nearby. There was a tranquillity about the place—even though it was in the open air. Quiet noises of the lapping water, rustling leaves and forest wildlife echoed around them.

'It's beautiful,' he whispered.

She smiled. 'Yes. Yes, it is.' She gestured towards the tea house. 'We call them *chashitsu*.' She pointed to a variety of exquisitely dressed women in traditional kimonos with their hair in intricate styles decorated with combs and ornaments. 'And these are the *teishu*, the host and teachers of the tea ceremony.'

He looked amazed. 'Are we going in there?'

'We are. Now, take your shoes off and…' she put her finger to her lips '…don't speak.'

The *teishu* met them at the door and gave a little bow. The floor was covered with tatami mats. She invited them to sit down and Katsuko sat cross-legged on the floor and Avery joined her.

She loved the tea ceremony but she enjoyed it even more as she watched Avery's face. She could see him itching to ask questions at every part of the ceremony. Even though it was called a ceremony it was more like a carefully choreographed dance.

The host ritually cleansed each item for the ceremony—the tea bowl, whisk and tea scoop, using prescribed motions, and then placed them in a precise order. The whisk was used to create a thin paste from water and a special type of powdered green Japanese tea called matcha. The paste was then whisked into a thick liquid.

This was the part of the ceremony that Katsuko loved. It was rhythmical, almost hypnotic, watching the liquid being whisked. Avery hardly moved. He was even breathing quietly as he watched everything intently. She slid her hand over next to his. He didn't even blink but must have sensed it was there because his warm hand covered hers. His thumb found its way under her palm where he stroked softly, sending a whole host of tingles up her arm. No. She'd never felt like this at a tea ceremony before.

When the tea was ready it was served in the tea bowl—the same tea bowl used by everyone. Bows were exchanged and Avery followed her lead. She raised the bowl as a gesture of respect to the host. Katsuko rotated the bowl, took a sip, complimented the host then wiped the rim of the bowl clean and passed it to Avery.

He mimicked her actions perfectly. He never even grimaced when he tasted the bitter tea.

When the ceremony was complete the *teisha* invited Avery to ask questions. And he did. More than Katsuko could ever have imagined. He'd paid attention to everything.

Every day this guy did something else to make her like him more.

An hour after the ceremony started it was finally complete. They emerged back out into the afternoon sun and had only taken a few steps when Katsuko's phone buzzed.

She pulled it from her pocket and sucked in a breath. 'Not again.'

Avery turned towards her. 'What? What is it?'

She paused, well aware that she was about to ruin a perfectly good day. 'I'm really sorry, but I'm going to have to go. It's my grandmother.'

'Is she sick?' There was instant concern on his face.

She gritted her teeth. If she were sick, things would be more straightforward. She gave a wry smile. 'Not sick, just cantankerous. She's flung her carers out. She does this on a regular basis.'

He half smiled. 'She what?'

Katsuko turned on the path to head back to the train station. 'It's like dealing with a toddler. At least I think it's like dealing with a toddler. Every now and then she throws her carers out and texts me to complain. What it means for tonight is that there's no one to make her dinner or get her ready for bed. I'll need to go and help.' She shook her head. 'Then I'll need to phone whoever she's insulted this time and apologise.'

Avery kept pace beside her. 'She does this a lot?'

'Oh, yes.' Katsuko was trying to calculate in her head the simplest way for Avery to get back to base. She pulled their tickets from her pocket.

'I'll tell you which line to get and where to change.'

He shook his head. 'No, you won't.'

She stopped walking. 'Why?'

He stuck his hands in his pockets and kept walking. 'Because I'm coming with you.'

She couldn't hide her surprise. 'What? No, you can't. I mean, you don't want to do that. You go back to base. I don't know how long I'll be. It's not fair.'

He slung his arm around her shoulder and pulled her closer. 'Life's not fair. Anyway, I want to meet your cantankerous old grandmother.'

Now she felt horrified. 'Why would you want to do that?'

He smiled down at her. 'I want to see if you've inherited any of her traits.'

CHAPTER SEVEN

As a doctor, Avery Flynn had met a lot of cantankerous patients in his time. But he'd never met anyone like Hiroko Satou. She definitely won the prize.

From the second they left their shoes at the entrance-way and entered her single-storey home he could sense the tension in the air. Not that he could understand a word of what was going on.

She didn't shout, but her tone spoke a thousand words. Katsuko tried to introduce him but he was instantly dismissed with one look. Then the tirade clearly aimed at Katsuko started.

Avery had never been rude, but as the staccato words flowed freely he started to get annoyed. It was clear Katsuko was doing everything she could to placate her grandmother, who clearly wasn't listening.

After about fifteen minutes Katsuko threw her hands in the air, walked through to the kitchen and started banging things around. She'd already warned him she'd need to make something for her grandmother's dinner.

He folded his arms and leaned against the wall. It could appear impertinent. But he was a twenty-eight-year-old man—not a boy—and now he could understand clearly why Katsuko had looked nervous on the way over.

The smell of food cooking quickly wafted from the kitchen. 'Can I do anything to help?' he asked.

There was a tiny rise of the old woman's eyebrows. Interesting. Katsuko had said she didn't speak or understand a word of English. Avery wasn't so sure.

'No, thanks' came the reply from the kitchen. 'She wouldn't like it.'

Avery caught the sharp gaze of the woman in the wheelchair currently scowling at him and gave her a knowing smile.

He started to walk slowly around the room. As expected, it was clutter-free with everything in easy reach. She had a giant modern television on the wall and her tablet sitting on the table next to her. It seemed she wasn't entirely steeped in tradition.

He stopped as he caught sight of a photograph in a frame on the wall. A beautiful young Japanese woman, around Katsuko's age, dressed in a traditional red kimono smiled back at him. The photo had aged a little around the edges. It had obviously been there for a while. He glanced around the rest of the room, looking for any photos of Katsuko. There were none.

'Your daughter was beautiful,' he said quietly. 'You must miss her.'

She blinked and her scowl deepened.

He kept walking. Her eyes occasionally darted towards the kitchen. She could hear Katsuko making dinner. Avery kept walking slowly, aware that the old lady's eyes were following his every move.

'Katsuko's a great nurse. A real credit to you.' He pointed to the photo. 'I can see she gets her beauty from her mother.' He paused. The old woman really did have an unwavering glare.

He faced her square on. 'You must be very proud of her.'

Finally, she drew her eyes off him, giving him a look

of disgust. She understood a whole lot more than she admitted to.

Katsuko stuck her head back through the doorway. 'Dinner will be ready soon. I'll just go and get her bed ready for later.' She crossed through the main room.

Avery leaned against the wall again. Hiroko Satou watched her granddaughter leave the room, then turned to glare at Avery again. He crossed one leg over the other and folded his arms. It was like a Mexican stand-off. But he wasn't afraid.

He could see the fury emanating from the old woman. In a lot of ways he felt sorry for her. Her gnarled hands were sitting on her lap. Her bare feet were visible under her blanket. The toe joints looked swollen and distended. Every bone in her body must ache. How many years must she have felt like this?

Had she been frustrated when she'd been unable to look after her granddaughter? Was that why she had such a poor relationship with the General?

But what was her excuse for the way she made Katsuko feel? There was no excuse for that.

He opened his mouth to speak again just as Katsuko came back into the room. Her grandmother started talking instantly, her eyes darting between Avery and Katsuko, her words low and fierce.

It took around ten seconds to realise that the latest rant was about him. Katsuko looked uncomfortable and she kept trying to answer, but her grandmother cut her off at every turn. It appeared that all her venom was now aimed at Avery.

He hated this. He had no clue what the words were, and he didn't care in the least that they were about him—all he cared about was the fact that Katsuko looked as though she was about to burst into tears.

If they were in the emergency department and a patient

or relative spoke to her like this, she wouldn't be long in putting them in their place. But here, in her grandmother's home, she looked the most vulnerable he'd ever seen her.

He straightened up and walked over to her, putting his arm around her waist. Every muscle in her body stiffened but he pretended he didn't notice. He was sending a clear message to the woman who was upsetting the woman he cared about.

'Let me help. What can I do?'

The words were simple but he hoped the look in his eyes told her a whole lot more. She stared up at him for a few seconds. Her brown eyes fixed on his and he could see her swallow nervously. 'Let me help you,' he urged.

Her grandmother spat out some more words and Katsuko blinked back tears before turning and going back into the kitchen. Two minutes later she appeared with a bowl of food for her grandmother.

Avery went into autopilot. He wheeled the chair over to the nearby table and positioned her carefully. Katsuko brought some chopsticks and a napkin for her grandmother and gestured for Avery to sit down at the other side of the room. A few seconds later she joined him. 'She doesn't like people watching her eat. She struggles to hold the chopsticks now.'

She stared down at her hands and he put his arm around her again, staring across at her grandmother defiantly. It was ridiculous. It made him feel like a teenager again, but he wasn't intimidated by the woman and he could see the affect she had on Katsuko. It was almost poisonous.

'Why do you come when she texts?'

Her eyes were wet. 'Who else would come?'

He pressed his lips together. 'I get that she's in pain. I get that she's from a different generation. But I'm struggling to see what you get from this relationship.'

She blinked in surprise. 'What does that mean? She's my grandmother.'

'She is. But you don't have to like her. And you don't have to jump when she texts.'

She shook her head in bewilderment. 'But then she'd have no one.' She sighed. 'I try not to. Sometimes I text back and tell her I'm at work. One time she threw her carers out seven days in a row.'

'Did she treat your mother like this?'

Her lips trembled. 'I remember lots of arguments. My father used to refuse to visit. He didn't want my mother to bring me here.'

'But here you are.'

He left the statement hanging between them.

There was so much he could say here. So much he wanted to say. But he wasn't sure how appropriate it was. It certainly wasn't appropriate to say it in her grandmother's house.

He took a deep breath and spoke quietly. 'As I've grown older I've realised the old adage that blood is thicker than water means nothing. You should surround yourself with people who love you—or no people at all. People who have a positive impact on your life.'

Her brow furrowed. 'Does that mean you don't see your family?'

A wave of sadness flooded over him. 'My parents aren't the best example of family. And my sister seems to have learned from their examples. The air force helps me keep a distance. It's my family now.'

Katsuko glanced over towards her grandmother. She'd finished her food, her slightly trembling hands were back in her lap and her eyes were closed. Katsuko reached over and laced her fingers through Avery's. 'That's sad,' she whispered.

'So is this,' he replied.

CHAPTER EIGHT

THE CATCALLING STARTED as soon he walked in.

'Woo-hoo, Captain Flynn, how are those kissable lips?'

'Hey, Avery, do you have a death wish or something?'

Frank walked past, shaking his head and tutting. 'The things some people will do to try and get a transfer out of here.'

Avery looked about, catching a few raised eyebrows. He walked down to the desk where the majority of the staff were standing.

'Well, if it isn't our very own Romeo,' said one of the nurses. The rest of the staff were laughing and looked at him in expectation. He felt a weird prickle go down his spine.

For the last few weeks he'd continued to see Katsuko on a regular basis. They weren't entirely keeping it a secret, he just hadn't discussed it with anyone he was working with.

And things had been a little awkward. After the visit to her grandmother's house Katsuko had pulled back. She hadn't said the words, but she'd been distant.

It should have dented his confidence but it hadn't. It wasn't his confidence he was worried about. It was hers. The visit to her grandmother's had taken the sparkle from her eyes and the shine from her confidence. He hated that—probably more than he should for a guy that was a temporary arrangement and only looking for some kind of fling.

Because he liked her. He liked her more and more. Their connection felt so real. She was feisty. She was good company. And she was sexy as hell. The perfect woman in every way. So why wasn't he telling the world they were dating? And why wasn't she?

He frowned at the faces around him. 'What on earth are you guys talking about?'

Glances were exchanged but no one spoke. Blake Anderson walked up behind him and gave him a slap on the back. 'Come with me, Captain Flynn. We need to have a chat about your risk-taking behaviour.'

He was smiling but there was seriousness behind his eyes. The rest of the staff found their voices again.

'You're in trouble now.'

'The plane leaves for Ohio in an hour.'

Avery had no idea what they were talking about. Risk-taking behaviour? Maybe in the past, but not recently. He followed Blake into his office and closed the door behind him.

'Are you going to tell me what all this is about?'

Blake looked at him carefully. 'No one has told you?'

'Told me what?' Avery looked over his shoulder. 'Is there a camera in here? Is this some kind of game show?'

Blake pulled his phone from his pocket. 'There isn't a camera in here, but there sure was one where you were a few weeks ago.' He touched the screen and turned the phone around. 'You really haven't seen this?'

Avery took the phone and tilted it to get a better view of the screen. It was like a movie. A film clip.

The view was high, as if taken from one of the street cameras. It was Hachiko Crossing at night, lit up by all the neon lights. One second the crossing was swarming with people, the next the camera zoomed in on a couple. A couple kissing in the middle of the crossing, just as it emptied and the lights were about to change.

Avery's breath caught somewhere in his throat.

There was no mistaking the couple. There was no mistaking his fedora.

And there was no mistaking the heat of the kiss.

He looked up at Blake. 'What on earth…?'

Blake still looked faintly amused. He folded his arms across his chest. 'Look at the caption.'

Avery scrolled back above the video clip. The words were written in English and—he presumed—Japanese: *Can you identify the mystery couple?*

He shook his head. 'But this was weeks ago. Who filmed it? I never saw anyone.'

He felt distinctly uncomfortable. Had Katsuko seen this? What would she say? Would she be happy or upset that people knew their relationship had developed? He played the clip again and tried to ignore the instant dryness in his throat. There was absolutely no mistaking his intentions with that kiss. He had one hand in her hair and the other firmly on her backside, pressing her against him.

Blake sighed. 'Check out the comments.'

Avery glanced underneath the video and blinked. More than a thousand comments. Then he looked at the views. *'What?'*

Blake held up his hands. 'It seems you're a bit of a slow burner. It appears that one of the street camera operators caught sight of your liaison and decided to post it, asking if anyone knows the couple. It's gone viral. People have been posting it all over. And if you scroll through the comments you'll see that some people have identified exactly who you both are…' he paused '…and which air force base you're from.'

Avery groaned. 'Oh, no.'

'Oh, yes.'

'I need to speak to Katsuko.'

'I think someone else is speaking to her—at least that's the impression I got when the General phoned me an hour ago.'

Avery cringed and closed his eyes for a second. 'What did he say?'

'You really want to know?' From Blake's tone it was apparent that, no, he really didn't want to know. 'Consider yourself spoken to about being a captain in the US Air Force and being caught on camera undertaking risky behaviour. You made it off that crossing with less than a second to spare.'

'I was kind of caught up.'

Blake smiled. 'I could see that.'

Something shot through Avery's mind. 'You only saw this an hour ago? How did everyone else see it?'

Blake shrugged. 'Coincidences, I imagine. I've got to assume you haven't been online this morning. I imagine you have a few messages waiting. Once you'd both been identified and tagged, the video clip circulated like wildfire among the staff.'

Avery groaned again. 'Great, just great.'

Blake gave him a serious stare. 'Avery, do me a favour, don't get caught on camera in future—I can't afford to be down one doctor.' He pressed his lips together for a second. 'And just so you know, she might be called firecracker but she's not as confident as you think. She's popular around here. Treat her badly and it won't just be the General you need to worry about.'

Something was wrong. It was her day off but she could hear the front door opening. Seconds later there was a shout. 'Katsuko?'

What on earth was Don doing home? He should be at

work. She rubbed her eyes and climbed out of bed, walking slowly out into the corridor and standing at the top of the stairs. He didn't look particularly happy.

'I'm off today.' She sighed. She'd never fall asleep again now. 'What's wrong?'

He gestured towards her. 'I need to speak to you. Come downstairs.'

She frowned. 'What? Can't this wait until later?'

He shook his head. 'No. It can't.'

By the time she got down the stairs Don had flipped open his laptop and had a video clip showing. Now she was really confused. She'd thought he wanted to talk to her.

'Watch' was all he said.

Two minutes later she had her head on the table. Shock. Embarrassment. And definitely cringeing.

'I think just about everyone on the base has seen this.'

'They have?' She didn't even ask where it had come from. She could find that out later.

'You were standing in the middle of the crossing. You barely made it off the street.'

She tried not to smile as memories of the kiss flooded through her.

'How do you think it reflects on this air base—on me—if members of our medical staff are seen behaving in a way that could put people at risk? What happens if the next big thing is people mimicking what you did? How long do you think it will be before one of those couples ends up the ER?'

She sat back in the chair. She wasn't normally a morning person and her patience was always short. Don was saying everything except what he really wanted to.

'It was only a kiss.'

'I'm not talking about the kiss.'

She stood up. 'Yes. Yes, you are. I'm twenty-five. I could be living in another country somewhere by now. I probably should be. It might surprise you exactly how many kisses I've had.'

He held up his hand. 'Too much information.'

She licked her lips and tried to let her befuddled brain make sense of things. 'I get it that you're not entirely happy about two members of base staff kissing in the middle of the busiest junction in the world. Believe me, it wasn't pre-planned. At least, not by me. I also get it that you might ask their supervisors to speak to them. But this isn't a big deal, Don. This isn't something you get reprimanded over.' She ran her fingers through her hair. 'So, if you want to ask me something about Avery, ask me.'

He raised his eyebrows and remained silent. It was difficult not to try and immediately fill the silence. Don had always been extremely good at this. It was one of his 'techniques'. He'd told her once he used it often—particularly when trying to get to the truth of an incident. People tended to panic and fill the silence with babble—babble that probably gave more away than they intended.

It might be first thing in the morning but Katsuko was far too smart for that. She raised her eyebrows back at him.

The corners of his mouth started to turn upwards. 'What do you know about Avery Flynn?'

She stepped forward and gave him a knowing nod. 'I guess that's the question I should be asking you. At this point, I imagine, you know his file off by heart.'

He blinked. Once.

'I like him.' There. She'd said it out loud.

Her stomach instantly churned. It wasn't entirely true. But only she knew that. She more than liked him. She just didn't know if she was ready to admit that.

Don was staring at her. She didn't move, didn't flinch—no matter how uncomfortable she felt. Sometimes it felt like those eyes could feel about in her brain and find the truth that she kept hidden. Like the time she'd sworn at a neighbour's kid, then said she hadn't. Or the time as a teenager she might have gone somewhere she shouldn't have. Don seemed to know everything.

'Only like him?'

Yep. He could see right into her brain. She thought for a second. 'I don't know. He makes me smile. I enjoy spending time with him. I intend to keep spending time with him.' She sucked in a deep breath. 'I took him to meet Hiroko.'

One eyebrow rose. 'Were you trying to determine his staying power?'

She smiled. 'Nothing like a cantankerous grandmother to scare a man off.'

'And has she?'

Katsuko paused, then shook her head as little pieces of the puzzle of Avery Flynn started to fall into place in her brain. 'Actually, not at all.'

Don gave a silent nod. 'What did you mean earlier?'

She was surprised at the subject change. She'd expected to be grilled on Avery—or at the very least asked for an introduction. She cringed as she realised he'd met her grandmother before he'd met Don. In hindsight that didn't seem quite right.

'Which part?'

Don looked serious. 'The part about living somewhere else?'

Had she said that out loud? Oh, no. That wasn't how she wanted to have this conversation. She wasn't even sure she was ready to have it yet. It had just been floating around inside her.

'I've been thinking. If I want to do well in the air force, if I want to get a promotion, I should probably think about serving on another base.'

Don moved around the table and picked up a pile of papers. Distraction technique. Thinking time.

He didn't meet her gaze. Just nodded as his eyes fixed on

the table. 'Yes, you probably should.' There was the tiniest waver in his voice and that broke her heart. Don wasn't her biological father, but she'd come to think of him that way. After a few years of staying with him she'd just started calling him Dad. It had seemed natural. It might be by default, but he'd become every bit as important to her as her own father had been. It had only been in the last few years, as an adult, that she'd occasionally called him Don again. He didn't seem to mind what she called him. Their relationship was that good, that steady, and she'd just hurt him.

Tears filled her eyes.

Don looked up. 'Where do you want to go?'

She shook her head and tried to blink back the tears. 'I haven't thought about it enough yet. I'd like to work somewhere I can get some different nursing experience.'

'You're bored with the ER?'

'I'll never be bored with the ER, but I need to grow as a nurse. Maybe I need to think about Theatres or ICU.'

Don opened his mouth to say something, then closed it again. Whatever it was, he must have reconsidered. 'Why don't we sit down sometime and look at the options?'

He was so matter-of-fact. So supportive. She walked over and put her hands around his neck and hugged him. She didn't do that much now. But she could tell he needed it. The man who'd practically given up his own life for her, manoeuvred a way to let them both remain in Japan, and supported her every step of the way was doing what every parent did at some stage—letting their child move on without them.

And after a few seconds Don hugged her back.

It was a weird kind of day. Some people were still shooting him strange glances. Some were cracking jokes to his face. There was even an occasional warning glance.

Katsuko had been a little strange when she'd come to

see him last night. After six weeks his house was finally starting to smell like something resembling normal. He'd bought around a hundred candles at a local market, all smelling of Japanese maple and jasmine, and had nearly burned them all. Katsuko hadn't even wrinkled her nose when she'd walked through his door last night.

But things had been a bit strained. Something was on her mind and she didn't seem to want to talk about it. She said the General had spoken to her but was fine.

Fine. What did that mean?

Tonight's night shift was slow. Which was unusual.

But it was a Tuesday. Did anything happen on a Tuesday? The other doctor on duty was due to sit exams so Avery had told him to hide out in the office with his books. Lily, the pregnant nurse, had looked a bit tired, so he'd sent her off to the staffroom to put her feet up for a while.

Katsuko had chatted casually, but had seemed very conscious that people were watching their every move so had managed to keep herself busy.

His stomach gave a little grumble so he stood up and stretched his back. 'Back in five, folks. I'm going to grab a sandwich.'

He strolled down the corridor, glancing from side to side. Katsuko was around here somewhere, maybe she'd join him for a coffee.

He pushed the door open.

And stopped thinking about food.

Lily was on the floor, having a seizure. Her arms and legs were jerking heavily.

'Help! I need help in here!' he shouted. Avery had never been a doctor who panicked. But a sudden wave swept over him.

What on earth…?

He was next to her in a second, turning her on to her side into the recovery position. She'd vomited, so he wiped at her mouth trying to maintain her airway. How long had she been doing this?

He glanced at his watch. It was important to time any seizure. He could only time it from the moment he'd found her, so that was where he'd start.

'Help!' he shouted again. Katsuko and Frank burst through the doors, complete confusion on their faces.

Katsuko's eyes were wide. 'Lily!' She ran over and dropped to her knees beside Avery. Frank turned on his heel and left.

'What on earth's wrong? She's been fine.'

Avery shook his head. Now he felt sick. He'd told her to come and rest earlier. She'd looked tired and had complained about her sore back. A pregnant woman nearing the end of her pregnancy. He hadn't thought any more than that.

'I have no idea. Has she complained about anything to you?'

Frank burst back through the doors, carrying a patient slide and pulling a trolley behind him. Two other members of staff were pale-faced behind him.

'We'll need to lift her onto the trolley, put this under her,' said Frank.

No one cared they were about to break all the health and safety rules about lifting patients from the floor. There wasn't time to go and find a proper patient hoist.

Avery was still trying to maintain Lily's airway. 'Anyone know anything about this? I thought Lily was well.'

'So did I,' said Katsuko quietly.

'Hold on.' Avery lifted his hand and everyone froze. The seizure seemed to be coming to an end, the jerking slowing.

'Wait until it's finished before we move her. I have no idea if she fell to the floor or slid from the chair. The last thing we need to do is drop her and cause any harm to her baby.'

When the jerking stopped he gave the signal and they

pulled her further onto her side and slid the patient slide underneath her. They had her on the trolley with the safety sides in place in only a few seconds.

Avery didn't even need to give the command. They took her straight to the resus room.

All the staff moved instantly. A blood-pressure cuff was put in place, her airway checked and an oxygen mask put on her face.

'I'll pull up her medical records,' said one of the admin staff. Avery gave her a grateful nod. She didn't normally come near the resus room but these were exceptional circumstances.

'I need to know what her last BP reading was. I need her last set of blood results and her last urine test. Shout them out when you find them, along with special notes from her obstetrician.'

'I'll contact her husband,' shouted someone else.

Katsuko took less than a minute to draw some bloods and insert a cannula. They'd need access to a vein if she started to fit again.

Now her airway was secure he walked around the bed and pulled off her shoes. Lily was wearing scrubs, the same as everyone else. He pulled up one trouser leg. And blinked.

Oedema. Lots of it. He pressed hard against her skin, trying to reach her ankle bone, and watched as the impression of his finger slowly filled again. Pitting oedema.

He pulled up her scrub top to get a look at her belly. 'Someone find me a foetal monitor—I need to check the baby.' He pressed his hands against her stomach. Oedema too.

'Why did we never notice any oedema?' he said out loud. He looked back at Lily's face. Did it look any different from normal? He didn't think so.

He reached for one of Lily's hands. She only wore her wedding ring. It was a little tight but not excessively so.

Her face and hands weren't obviously swollen like her abdomen and legs.

'What's the BP?' His eyes glanced at the monitor.

'One-eighty over one-fifteen.'

There were anxious glances around the room. Avery turned to Katsuko and spoke in a low voice. 'Find me her obstetrician. I don't care what time of the night it is.'

He turned to the rest of the staff. 'We have to treat this as eclampsia. I need a magnesium sulphate infusion to help prevent more seizures and some IV hydralazine for her blood pressure. Let's get Lily stabilised.'

Hardly anyone spoke. All the staff were too shocked. Everyone kept their heads down and moved on automatic pilot. Avery felt a bit like that himself. He'd only been here six weeks, some of the staff here would have worked with Lily for years. He couldn't even imagine how they were feeling.

Katsuko walked back in, her expression serious. She handed him the phone. 'Her obstetrician, Dr Tanaka, is on the other side of Tokyo. He's more than an hour away. Can you talk to him?'

Avery looked around the room again. This time it was a shout of pure frustration. 'Did someone find me a foetal monitor?'

Someone scurried from the room. He grabbed the phone from Katsuko's hand and walked to the doorway, out of earshot of the rest of the staff. Luan, the doctor who'd been studying earlier, appeared wide-eyed in front of him. Avery gestured over his shoulder. 'I need to speak to Lily's obstetrician. Keep an eye on her.'

He waited until Luan was inside the room, then pressed the phone to his ear and leaned back against the wall. He kept his voice low. 'Dr Tanaka? You'll need to help me out here. I'm an emergency physician. I've delivered two babies in the last seven years and both of them virtually fell into my hands.'

He didn't have time to be coy. He knew basic obstetrics but he was by no means an expert. Some doctors didn't like to admit that they didn't know everything. Avery wasn't that foolish. A staff member's—and her baby's—life could be on the line here.

Even Dr Tanaka sounded panicked while he spoke. 'Tell me what you've done.'

'Lily was seizing when I found her. She'd previously said she was getting tired and her back was sore. She has widespread oedema on her legs and abdomen but not her hands and face. She's hypertensive, one-eighty over one-fifteen. I've started her on magnesium sulphate and given her a bolus of hydralazine.'

He heard Dr Tanaka suck in a sharp breath. 'Give me a second. I'm pulling up her notes. Okay. There have been no problems with this pregnancy. It's been straightforward. Lily had two miscarriages before this, but no other history of note. I saw her around ten days ago. BP normal, urine clear. I examined her—there was no oedema.' He took another breath. 'Lily's a nurse. She's an intelligent woman. This has to have been sudden onset. A little lower leg oedema in late pregnancy wouldn't be alarming. She's currently just over thirty-five weeks and was due to see me again in a couple of days. I think, at this stage, we have to consider HELLP syndrome. Tell me about the baby.'

Avery let out the breath he'd been holding. HELLP syndrome. Not what he wanted to hear. Haemolysis, elevated liver enzymes and low platelet count. It could be life threatening for both mother and baby.

There was a hand on his shoulder. Katsuko held up the foetal monitor. 'Do you want me to do this?'

He could hear the waver in her voice. She was scared. Scared that something bad was about to happen to her colleague. He shook his head. 'Give me a minute,' he said into the phone as he handed it to Katsuko. 'Talk to Dr Tanaka.'

As he strode back into the room he felt like all eyes were on him. The foetal monitor wasn't the most modern he'd ever seen but then again this wasn't an obstetrician's office. All he needed to do right now was find a heartbeat.

He switched on the monitor and put his hands on Lily's abdomen again, trying to establish the lie of the baby. He turned the sound up on the monitor. The room instantly quietened.

He pressed the monitor to Lily's swollen stomach and held his breath.

Nothing.

He adjusted the position and pushed back the horrible little surge of panic. Doctors didn't panic. They just didn't.

Still nothing. Did this thing even work?

'Dr Tanaka says he's found a family history of eclampsia in Lily's notes. Both her mother and aunt suffered from it.'

Perfect. Just perfect.

He pressed harder.

Finally. A heartbeat. The wave of relief only lasted a few seconds. He checked the reading on the monitor. One-eighteen.

He walked back to the doorway and took the phone from Katsuko. He kept his voice low. 'Foetal bradycardia. One hundred and eighteen beats per minute.'

'That's not unexpected with eclampsia and HELLP syndrome, particularly after a seizure,' said Dr Tanaka. 'It could also be due to the magnesium sulphate. You'll need to keep monitoring closely. Have you taken bloods?'

'Yes, they're done.'

'Good, in that case find an anaesthetist to assess Lily. I'm leaving now. If this is HELLP syndrome we'll need to deliver the baby as soon as possible. Keep monitoring her blood pressure and the baby.'

Avery listened to a few more instructions before finally hanging up. Katsuko was at his side in an instant. 'Are you okay?'

'Are you?'

She closed her eyes for just a second, then opened them again, pushing her shoulders down and meeting his gaze. 'I have to be. *We* have to be.'

We.

He knew what she was saying. He knew that she didn't really mean *that.* And while he'd always been an attentive and caring boyfriend, as soon as any ex had started referring to them as *we* it had sent uncomfortable prickles down his spine and he'd looked forward to shipping out.

He'd never made promises of for ever because he just didn't believe in them. They didn't exist. Oh, the start of every relationship was good. The honeymoon period when you wanted to see someone as much as possible and just the fact they walked in the room could make you smile.

But it never lasted. At least it hadn't for his mother, father or sister. Why should he be any different?

But this time he didn't have uncomfortable prickles. He didn't have that horrible worry of letting someone down.

Even though the resus room was the busiest room in the ER, no one was looking at them. Everyone was focusing on Lily—just the way they should.

He reached forward and threaded his fingers through Katsuko's. Something about touching her felt completely natural. Felt like the thing that he was supposed to do. 'Let's get through this,' he said quietly. 'We're not leaving until Lily and her baby are safe.'

Katsuko nodded. 'Let's do this.'

Lily's husband was distraught. Avery had spoken to him calmly and with an assurance Katsuko knew he didn't really have. 'I told her to stop work,' he said, shaking his head. 'I told her it was time to rest and forget about work.'

'Did she complain of anything except being tired and having a sore back?'

Lily's husband nodded. 'She's felt sick the last two days. She was joking about the morning sickness being back. And she was uncomfortable. She had a weird kind of pain around her right side. And she had a bit of a headache last night that wouldn't shift.'

Katsuko shot a glance at Avery. Everything fitted with the guidelines she'd pulled up for HELLP syndrome. It wasn't something she'd seen in the ER before. Last time she'd encountered this she'd been doing a student placement in a labour ward. She held out her hand towards Lily's husband. She'd known them both for a few years. 'Come on, Luke. Let me take you to see her. The obstetrician will be here any minute and I suspect you're going to meet your baby soon after that.'

She led him down the corridor to the resus room and put her arm around him when he seemed to crumple. Frank found a chair and said lots of reassuring words. There had been no more seizures and Lily's blood pressure had started to drop just a little.

Two hours later Lily and her husband had a baby son. Protocols stated that because a member of staff had become unwell on duty, Blake Anderson had to be called. He took the decision to call in the next shift early and send everyone else home.

'We'll debrief tomorrow, folks. It's always hard when it's one of our own. Let's give Lily and her husband some time and space to recover. Then we can all celebrate the new arrival.'

They were carefully optimistic words. Lily had been transferred to the ICU. There was still a chance she could go into organ failure. They just had to hope and pray that she didn't.

Katsuko gave a grateful nod and headed to the changing room. Five minutes later she was searching for Avery.

Fifteen minutes later she was still searching. One of the cleaners finally gave her some hope. 'I think I saw him heading towards the vending machines.'

She headed down the corridor. It was in darkness, and only the dim lights from the machines let her notice a pair of white runners sticking out.

'Avery? Is that you?'

She hurried down the corridor.

It was definitely Avery. He was slumped halfway against the back wall and the side of one of the machines. His eyes looked half-glazed. She crouched down. 'Avery? Are you okay?'

She reached forward and touched his hand. He looked up.

Those eyes. Those pale green eyes that had mesmerised her right from the beginning. Those confident, cocky pale green eyes that seemed to both taunt her and flirt with her at the same time. They didn't look like that tonight.

She flung her bag to the side and knelt on the floor. 'Avery? What's wrong?' She shuffled a little towards him. His permanently too-long hair was ruffled in every direction but the right one. 'Honey?'

His eyes connected with hers. He looked exhausted. Completely exhausted.

She grabbed his hand and pulled him forward. 'What's wrong?'

He shook his head. 'Nothing.' Then gave her a dopey smile as he lifted up his other hand and shrugged. 'Everything. I was hungry. I just came in here to find some food. That's what I was doing when I found Lily.'

She froze. It was the way he'd said her name. She got it. She really got it.

'Come on, Avery. You're exhausted. It's been a horrible

shift for us all. But you were the doctor in charge. Everything was on your shoulders.' She reached forward and ran her fingers through his hair. 'You need to get some sleep.'

She pulled at his arm a little more, bringing him closer to her.

He gave his head a shake. 'I just sat down for a second.'

She smiled. 'I know. I get it. I've been there. But let's go. This isn't the best place to hang out.'

He pushed himself up and she grabbed hold of him. 'Do you have any food in the house?'

He frowned and then nodded, giving her a curious look. 'Why?''

She touched his cheek. 'Because I'm going to make you something to eat.'

He paused and let out the longest breath. 'Kat—'

She held up her hand. 'Whatever it is, it can wait. You did good today. We all did good.'

He shook his head, then spun around unexpectedly and took a kick at one of the vending machines. It rocked backwards and forwards for a few seconds.

He didn't shout but the voice that came out was one of pure and utter frustration. 'I didn't! Why didn't I notice something was wrong with Lily? What if I hadn't walked into the coffee room when I did? She'd vomited. She could have choked. Anything could have happened.' The worry lines on his forehead were so deep and she could practically see the thoughts churning around his head. Both hands pushed against the glass of the machine, then his head sagged down against it.

She was stunned. She'd never seen him like this. The whole time she'd been in that resus room she'd been giving silent prayers of thanks that Avery was the doctor on duty. She trusted him. She had faith in him.

She reached out and touched his shoulder.

'Well, if you missed it, so did her obstetrician. So did I.

So did Frank. So did Samuru. So did everyone on duty tonight. And so did Lily. You heard Dr Tanaka. He thinks it was very rapid onset. It can happen.' She pulled him around to face her and clasped his hand. 'I heard you. I heard you tell Dr Tanaka that you'd only delivered two babies in the last seven years. You were totally out of your comfort zone tonight and I think I was the only one that noticed.'

He shook his head and ran his fingers through his hair. 'You have no idea how much I was out of my comfort zone. And it's ridiculous. I've treated bomb injuries. Even though I'm not a surgeon I've ended up in Theatre more times than I care to remember. I've seen hundreds of kids even though I'm not a paediatrician. If I had a dollar for every MI or chest infection I've diagnosed, I'd be a millionaire. But obstetrics?' He shook his head. 'I've hardly seen any cases.' He paused for a moment. 'Lily spoke to me last week about how happy she was and how much she was looking forward to this baby. She couldn't wait to be a mother. When I thought that might slip away today and it was all in my hands...'

He stared off into the distance. Katsuko put her arms around his neck, staring up into his eyes. She kept her voice low. 'When you shouted me through to the coffee room and I saw Lily fitting on the floor I thought I was going to be sick. When you didn't find a heartbeat straight away I thought I was going to be sick again. When Dr Tanaka said he was over an hour away I wanted to cry.'

His gaze met hers. There it was. The flash of recognition in his eyes. He nodded in appreciation, then said slowly, 'But this is our job, Katsuko. This is the life that we've chosen. I just hate it that I didn't know everything in there.'

He looked so racked with guilt that her heart squeezed. She leaned forward and kissed his cheek, her lips coming into contact with his stubbled jaw. 'Avery, I'm sure I've heard of HELLP syndrome but I could barely remember what to do. I heard you. You spoke to the obstetrician straight away and were completely honest with him. The treatment you'd started was correct. You did nothing wrong. Lily was in good hands. Lily was in safe hands. That first hour was crucial.'

He ran his fingers through his hair again. 'But what if she ends up in organ failure? It's still a possibility. She isn't out of the woods yet.'

Katsuko nodded. 'I know she isn't, but if we go upstairs now we'll just get in the way. Blake told us all to go home. That's what we need to do.'

His stomach growled loudly in protest and she let out a laugh and threaded her fingers through his. She was a nurse. She was used to taking care of people. But she wasn't on air force time now. She was on her own. And this was the first time she'd been absolutely sure about her next step.

Avery wasn't dating her because she was the General's daughter. Avery wasn't looking for promotion. Avery wasn't trying to win friends and influence people. Avery was just a guy, trying to do the best job that he could.

And it was quite possible she loved him for it.

'How about a little company?'

He blinked. Then his gaze narrowed a little as if he was trying to work out what she was saying. 'What kind of company?'

She licked her lips and met his gaze. She wasn't embarrassed. It didn't feel awkward. It felt completely natural.

'Overnight company.' Her words were assured.

He put his hands on her hips and leaned back a little. 'Katsuko, did you just proposition me?'

He was teasing her again. He was starting to get back to normal.

She stood on tiptoe. 'So, what if I did?'

He grinned. 'What if you get seen leaving the Captain's house first thing in the morning?'

She placed her hands on his chest. 'I've no intention of being seen leaving the Captain's house first thing in the morning. I'm planning on sleeping late and having breakfast in bed.'

He slipped his arm around her waist as they started walking back along the corridor. 'What do you eat for breakfast?'

She slapped his arm. 'Eggs. You'd better have some.'

He stopped walking and pulled a face. 'Oops.'

'And obviously I'll want my favourite coffee.'

'I don't think I can whip up a skinny vanilla latte with my poor kitchen supplies.'

'What exactly do you have in your cupboards and fridge?'

He smiled. 'I have some sushi, a can of beans and some beer.'

She shook her head and wagged her finger at him. 'Watch out. I expect to get exactly what I want.'

He picked her up and twirled her round. The twinkle in his eye that she was used to was back. 'I'm sure I'll be able to give you exactly what you want.'

'Promises, promises.' She pushed open the door. 'How about a wager?'

He raised his eyebrow. 'I like the sound of that. What's the wager?'

She looked around. 'Oh, I've left my jacket by the vending machine. Can you grab it?'

'Sure,' he said. He walked back down the corridor quickly and she didn't even try to hide her smile.

'Avery, the wager?'

He bent to pick up her jacket. 'Yes?'

'Last one back to your place has to do the coffee run in the morning.'

And with that she winked and raced out into the dark night.

CHAPTER NINE

'CAPTAIN FLYNN, WILL you report to the Major General's office, please?'

Avery nearly choked on the cup of coffee that he'd just taken a drink from.

'Of course. I'll be there directly.'

He stood up and looked around. He was dressed in scrubs so he'd need to change into his uniform.

He stuck his head around the door of Blake's office. 'Blake, I've been told to go to the General's office.'

Blake looked up. It was obvious he was trying not to grimace. 'Any idea what about?'

Avery shook his head. 'Not a clue.'

Except for the fact I've been seeing his daughter ever since I got here.

Everyone knew. They didn't even try to hide it. Katsuko had stayed over at his house on more than one occasion. The last month had been a steep learning curve. He'd learned how to make her the coffee she liked. He'd learned not to wash her delicate underwear with his uniforms. He'd learned that she mumbled in her sleep. But most of all he'd learned just how much he enjoyed being around her. She was feisty. She was smart. And loved to laugh. And sometimes she was vulnerable.

If he was working a shift and she wasn't on duty he'd

started to look at the clock and count the minutes until he could see her again. Part of him wanted to tread warily—he'd never really been like this before. But the other part of him just wanted to enjoy it.

'Better hurry along, then,' quipped Blake. 'I'll cover your patients.'

It only took five minutes to change, then another ten to walk across the base to the General's office. He was a grown man having an adult relationship with a grown woman. So why did he feel like a teenage boy?

He'd never actually met the General. Katsuko had made a few vague noises about them meeting at some point but it hadn't been an issue he'd laboured. He just hadn't expected to get called to the General's office.

There was no way he was going to act nervous. He pushed his shoulders back and held his head high as he entered.

The General's secretary looked up and smiled. 'Captain Flynn? Good. I have something for you.'

She stood up and walked to a table behind her and picked up a large envelope.

Avery glanced at the General's door. It was closed. No sounds. Maybe he wasn't even in?

The secretary held out a log book for him to sign. She handed the envelope over with a rueful look. 'It seems like this has taken a while to get to you. It seems to have been halfway around the world.'

She wasn't kidding. His name and rank, along with various base addresses, had been crossed out and rewritten on the front of the ragged envelope.

He looked at the return address. An attorney firm in New York. He'd never heard of them. There was an uneasy pang in his stomach. Was he being sued for something? Doctors did get sued for malpractice, but he'd never had any complaints raised.

He held up the envelope. 'Is this it?'

The secretary smiled and nodded. 'That's it, Captain.' She sat back down in her chair and carried on working.

Part of him was relieved. The General didn't want to see him at all. It was nothing to do with the General.

He walked outside and tore open the envelope, pulling out the papers inside.

As executors of the estate of the late Stuart Elijah Flynn, we are acting on behalf of our client, previously undeclared dependant Mary Elizabeth Flynn...

Who?

It was like a blast from the past. No one brought up Uncle Stuey's name any more—only him. His eyes scanned the rest of the letter. There. A date of birth. A daughter? Uncle Stuey had had a daughter? Since when?

He kept reading. According to this letter—which had taken nearly a year to reach him—Uncle Stuey had fathered a child twenty years ago in Brazil. It appeared that the daughter had only found out who her father was when her mother had become unwell and had since put in a claim on the estate.

What estate?

There was also a request for a DNA sample from himself to assist verification of the familial links.

He couldn't believe it. He couldn't believe a single word of it. The one person in his family he'd actually respected. The one person he'd actually looked up to had refused to acknowledge the birth of his daughter.

He could feel fury build inside him as he stalked back towards the ER.

'Avery! Avery! What are you doing? I thought you were on duty?'

Katsuko came running up behind him, her hair pulled back from her face and her swimming bag on her shoulder.

'I am.' He kept walking.

'Hey,' she said, tugging at his arm. 'What's wrong?'

He paused and thrust the letter towards her. 'It seems that Uncle Stuey had a daughter he'd never acknowledged. She's put a claim on his estate.'

'What?' Katsuko looked horrified. She started to scan the letter but couldn't stop the barrage of questions. 'How do you know he never acknowledged her?'

'Well, I've never actually heard of her.'

Katsuko screwed up her face. 'When was she born? Twenty years ago? How long is it since your uncle died?'

Avery stopped walking. 'Just short of twenty years ago.'

'Then did he even know about her?'

Avery took a breath. That hadn't even occurred to him—probably because he hadn't been thinking straight.

'Brazil? Was that one of the places your uncle visited? And how do you even know she's your uncle's daughter?' Her voice climbed in pitch and she stopped walking. 'They want you to do a DNA test?'

She shook her head. 'Avery, this is crazy.'

He pulled his hat off his head. 'I know. I can't believe it. Uncle Stuey was the one person I thought had got life right.'

Katsuko wrinkled her nose. 'Even though he "acquired" artefacts he probably shouldn't have?'

It was a valid question. And one that he'd spent most of his life ignoring. He waved his hand. 'I've never really looked into all that. I was young at the time. And my father has never wanted to discuss the details of what Uncle Stuart really did. I only have what I can remember.'

'Then let me ask the key question.'

'What's that?'

'The estate. This is all about inheritance. Did your uncle leave you anything and if he did, is there anything left?'

The realisation hit Avery like a bolt of lightning. Money. Of course. These were attorneys. This was actually about money.

He let out a laugh. 'After all these years someone wants money from Uncle Stuart? Well, it's long gone. He left me some money to help pay for college and medical school. All I've got left now is his fedora.' He shook his head. 'And I'm not handing that over to anyone.'

'I don't get it. Isn't she far too late anyway? Doesn't the statute of limitations apply?'

Avery pointed to the bottom paragraph of the letter. 'I have no idea. They're talking about a discovery rule and something about probate. It doesn't matter anyway. There's nothing to claim.'

Katsuko reached over and put her hand on his arm. 'Then why are you getting so worked up over this?'

The tension that had been building inside him bubbled over. 'Because of that!' He pointed at the letter. 'The implication in it. It destroys the memory of the man that I knew. The only good memories I have of my family are the ones of Uncle Stuart. He was my one hope that I wouldn't grow up to be like my father or my mother. You know that old nature versus nurture debate?'

She nodded.

'Well, I don't win on any count. Uncle Stuart was the last chance that the family genes might actually be okay.'

Katsuko took a deep breath and looked away. He hadn't meant to shout but he hated everything about this. He hated to be blindsided and this had been totally unexpected. No one had ever mentioned that Uncle Stuey had had any love interests. Avery couldn't ever remember his uncle talking about a girlfriend or anything like it. Everything had always been about the excitement of his job.

He frowned. But why would a grown man talk about adult relationships with a nine-year-old?

'You know what?'

Katsuko's words snapped him away from his thoughts.

Her brown eyes were flashing. She looked mad. 'I get it that you're annoyed about someone slighting your uncle. And I know that lots of families have issues. But you still have your parents—both of them. You still have a family that you could choose to fit into if you want to.'

Were those words supposed to make him feel guilty?

'And you have the General. And your grandmother. But you don't want to visit her, do you?'

She stepped back as if she'd been stung.

He shook his head. 'You have no idea what they're like, Katsuko. After ten minutes my father would probably be trying to date you, my mother would probably be trying to date Don, and my sister would be trying to con you into giving her a credit card.'

He threw up his hands. 'I mean, what am I even doing here—with you? No one in my family has ever had a relationship that worked out. My father has been married four times—each marriage more ridiculous than the one before. Any day now he'll reach number five. My mother just looks for the next rich, eligible bachelor and my sister is going exactly the same way. Uncle Stuey was the only person who gave me hope—and now I wonder why. He didn't even have any relationships with anyone that I knew about.' He stopped dead and looked her straight in the eye. 'I can't give you what you want, Katsuko. I can't give you what you need, or what you deserve. My family track record says it all. I'll be gone soon and you have a career to build. You can do better. You can do better than me. Go and find him.'

The words were out. He didn't want to mean any of them. But he had to be honest with her. He had to tell her what he was. What type of family he was a part of. What could he really offer her?

He wanted to be so much more than the sum of what he thought he was. Did genes really play a part in who you were? Could he ever hope to have any kind of loving, normal relationship?

She worried so much about fitting in. The truth was, it was the other way round. His family would never fit with the beliefs and ideals she had in her head.

He wasn't good enough for her. His family wasn't good enough for her.

Katsuko looked away. It was clear she was still upset. Her hands were shaking.

He hated himself right now. He wanted to put his arms around her and promise her that he would do his best for her. But would that ever be good enough? Right now, he wasn't sure.

She stared at the ground for a few seconds, then spoke quietly. 'I guess you'd better get back to work.'

Silence filled the air between them. He'd been too blunt. He hadn't meant to hurt her. His mind flew back to that first night when she'd run her finger over the picture of her mother and father.

He ran his fingers through his hair. 'Look, I'm sorry.'

She gave a nod. 'So am I.' And turned and strode away.

The words played on his mind for the rest of the day. He was mad with himself. It was almost as if he was trying to push her away. Why would he do that?

No matter what he did, he couldn't get Katsuko out of his head.

She was there. She was there to stay.

He'd met her grandmother. She was impossible. It didn't matter that he couldn't speak Japanese. The language she spoke was pretty universal.

There was no love or compassion in her eyes for her granddaughter. And Katsuko certainly hadn't acted like the *faiyakuraka* she was nicknamed after at work. In her grandmother's presence she was meek.

Some people might call it respectful, and in a way it was. But she shouldn't need to hide her personality and nature from her grandmother. He'd hated the expression in her eyes as she'd run after her grandmother. She was a nurse, caring was in her nature, being downtrodden was not.

He wondered if he'd experienced a little of what Katsuko's father and then Don had. It lit a little fire inside him.

His fists clenched as he sat at the computer screen at work. He shouldn't be wearing green scrubs, he should be dressed as a Neanderthal. That was how he felt. He wanted to protect her. Let her know how much she was valued. Let her know how much she was loved.

His hands sprang apart—the fists lost. His skin prickled and he looked down. This was the first time he wasn't looking forward to the end of a posting. In fact, he was secretly dreading the fact he didn't even know how long he'd be here. The commander of the medical service had already let him know that because of his willingness to step in at the last minute with no fuss or complaint, his next posting was his call. But did he really want to leave at all?

Katsuko had already spoken about looking at other postings. He should be excited for her—some of the places she was considering he'd already worked in. Now he was doing something he'd never done before. Instead of thinking about facilities and new experiences all the different bases had to offer, he was thinking about miles. And the distance that could be between them. And that was brand new for him.

He'd never tried a long-distance relationship. He'd never wanted to. But now, all of a sudden, it was definitely on his mind. Lots of colleagues in the forces had long-distance relationships. They had to. Families couldn't go to some bases. If husbands, wives or children had certain medical conditions it could mean they were deemed unsuitable to live in some bases with restricted facilities. Husbands, wives and families could be apart for months—and with his family history, what made him think he could even be cut out for that?

He hated these doubts. He hated feeling like this. He hadn't even sat down and had this conversation with Katsuko yet—the *What about the future?* conversation. It terrified him.

He'd proved that earlier when he'd blurted out the most stupid words he could possibly have said.

He thought about the expression on her face, the foolish words he'd said to hurt her. Why do that to someone that you loved?

Love. The thing that his father claimed to be permanently in or out of. Love. What he'd seen in the eyes of Jay Lim's parents when they'd seen each other again. Love. It practically emanated from the photo that Katsuko had of her parents.

He'd always assumed it would never work for him. He'd never really had a reason to think differently.

But now he did. And that reason was Katsuko.

He leaned forward and put his head in his hands and groaned. How on earth could he make things right?

He had to make a phone call. He had to deal with things back home—things in the past—if he could ever hope to build a future.

He stood up quickly, making his wheeled chair skid across the floor. He had to try and take some control back. And he knew where to start.

Seiko, one of the aerospace medical technicians, was restocking the emergency trolley. He walked over. 'Seiko? Have you got a minute?'

She looked up and nodded. 'Do you need help with a patient?'

He shook his head. It didn't matter that this news would

probably spread like some crazy infectious disease around the department. 'I need some help with some Japanese words. If I tell you what I want to say, would you write it down for me and help me with the pronunciation?'

She gave a nod. 'No problem.'

Wait until I tell you what I want translated.

It was time to make a start—and the sooner, the better.

He dialled the number and waited impatiently for the phone to ring.

After the longest time his father picked up. 'Dad, it's Avery.'

There was a silence. 'To what do I owe this honour?'

He winced but wasn't really surprised. After the last visit he'd kept contact to a minimum. There was no point in trying to make small talk. 'I've been contacted by a firm of attorneys.'

'What have you done?'

Avery sighed. '*I* haven't done anything. Have you heard of a Mary Elizabeth Flynn?'

'Who?'

Avery hesitated. He wasn't quite sure how to say this. 'She claims to be Uncle Stuey's kid.'

His father let out a raucous laugh. 'Another one? Well, they're all coming out of the woodwork now.'

Avery shifted uncomfortably. 'What's that supposed to mean?'

'So where's this one from, then?'

'She's from Brazil. But the attorney letter was sent nearly a year ago. It seems to have ping-ponged around every air force base trying to find me.'

'A year ago? She'll long since have given up. Bet she's changed her name to something else by now.'

'Dad, what are you talking about? What did you mean, they're all coming out of the woodwork?'

His father made a strange slurping noise. Great, he was drinking again. Avery glanced at his watch and tried to work out what time it was back in the US.

'How long has it been since you were home?' his father asked.

That didn't require much thought. Even though his father's reference to home and Avery's reference to home were two different things. 'More than a year ago. More like sixteen months.'

'Ah, you missed all the fun, then.'

'What fun?'

'One of the crazy cable TV stations made a documentary about Stu. It was one of those hunt-the-artefact kind of things. Some of what they said was true and some of what they said was complete and utter rubbish. They interviewed me. I think they wanted to interview you too at the time but you weren't around.'

Avery was getting impatient. 'Dad, what happened?'

His father laughed. 'You know television. They made it all mysterious. Lots of mist and references to lost treasure. They made out that Stuey had stolen a whole host of artefacts from all around the world and had been a secret billionaire. About two weeks later the letters started pouring in.'

'What letters?'

'Like the one you got. Lost children, some of whom had mysteriously changed their names by deed poll two days after the show. It was all a lot of hocus pocus.'

'So none of this is true?'

'Of course it's not true.'

He should feel reassured but he couldn't be. He'd never heard of this TV show. Plus his father was obviously drinking. 'How can you be sure? Uncle Stuey spent his life wandering the globe. There is a chance he could have children he didn't know about.'

His father's tone changed. It was almost as if he was looking over his shoulder to see who was listening. 'I know there's no possibility that Uncle Stuey could have kids. He had mumps as a child. There was no chance of children. Why do you think he left your mother and went halfway around the globe? He couldn't stand the fact that she married me instead. You were the son he always wanted.'

An arctic breeze swept over Avery. 'Uncle Stuey went out with Mom?'

'Of course he did. But your mom wanted a family and after he had mumps there was no chance of that. He decided that exploration and archaeology were his new profession—got a job with the museum and never looked back. He only ever really came back to see you.'

Avery's head was swimming. He'd never heard any of this. He'd never noticed anything weird between his mother and uncle. How could he have missed this?

'Why didn't you ever tell me any of this?'

'What did it matter? Your mother and I were never really suited.'

Avery leaned back against the wall. Part of him felt relieved that his Uncle Stuey wasn't some old-fashioned kind of cad and part of him felt sorry for the man who'd had to watch the woman he loved marry his brother.

'So, none of this is true? I can just destroy the letter?'

'That's what we did with all the rest. We did have one persistent attorney who decided we must have secretly hidden all of Uncle Stuey's artefacts. He tried to serve us with something or other.'

Avery shook his head. 'What was it?'

'Who knows? Who cares?' His father kept talking but Avery stopped listening. Other thoughts were flooding through his mind. How must his uncle have felt?

It was bad enough that mom had married his father. But when their marriage had failed and she'd immediately zoned in on any man with money it must have made him feel even worse. First she'd wanted kids. Then she'd wanted money.

His parents had ping-ponged from one bad relationship to another. And for the first time in his life he could finally understand why.

But that was them.

That wasn't him.

His sister might be following their example, but he didn't have to.

Uncle Stuey was still exactly the person he'd thought he was. In fact, he was more. He'd loved someone and walked away to let her have the life she'd thought she'd wanted.

And he'd stayed away to ensure he didn't influence the relationship any more than he should. Avery's heart gave a squeeze. His memories of his uncle were even more precious than before.

'I have to go, Dad,' he said quickly. 'I'll call you some other time.'

He sat down for a second, the battered envelope still in his hands.

It was amazing what some people would do for money. He was mad. He wanted to ring the legal firm and tell them exactly what he thought of them and their client. But that would achieve nothing.

He had too much else to think about.

He pulled another piece of paper from his pocket. The scribbled words that Seiko had written for him. She'd only slightly raised her eyebrows when Avery had asked her to translate a few things for him.

The question was—what would he do with them?

Katsuko was sitting at the table with a whole host of printouts in front of her. Every base. Every hospital. Every facility.

There was a whole world of opportunity out there. She just hadn't had the chance to explore it. She'd made herself a checklist, narrowing down what specialities were listed.

Then she pulled up a blog site for air force personnel. This way she could find out the more informal things. Where did other staff recommend? Were there places that had difficult reputations? What were the chances of having her request accepted at particular bases?

She put down her pen. Avery. He'd told her to go ahead. To make plans without him. The words had been awful, but the pain in his eyes had been worse. Did he really think he wasn't good enough for her?

She wasn't even sure if she should be thinking this way. But Avery Flynn had managed to creep under every defence system that she had. She'd known his position here was temporary. They'd never really discussed anything long-term. But she'd never really wanted to discuss anything long-term before.

She stared down at the papers. If she could just live her life in the bubble that was Okatu base, that would be fine. She'd still have Don. She'd still have the place she'd grown up in and she'd still have her friends.

But life was changing around her. She wanted more. She wanted to sit down and look at her career and see what should come next. She wanted to think about the future.

What had hurt most were his words today. They'd affected her in a way she hadn't expected. How could so few words make her feel like her feet had just been swept away from her?

It had been a simple squabble. She knew that. She just hadn't been ready for the impact.

It had been their first argument—and it hadn't even really been that. All couples argued. That was normal. And it didn't matter that he'd apologised by text a little while later, telling her he wanted to see her. He wanted to talk to her. The topsy-turvy feeling in her stomach hadn't shifted.

And it wouldn't shift until she saw him again and he put his arms around her.

She kind of hated the fact that another person had the ability to affect her feelings and emotions. Her grandmother had done it on a regular basis since she'd been a child. But never had a man.

Her grandmother. She gulped and stared at the papers again. She could only imagine what her grandmother would say if she told her she was being posted elsewhere. What would happen if her grandmother messaged her while she was on another continent, telling her that something was wrong? Who would help her?

She could hardly ask Don. He couldn't bear to be in her grandmother's presence. Was this really the right time to go?

Wine. She needed wine right now.

The doorbell rang and her heart gave a little leap. Was it that time already?

Avery opened the door with a bottle of white wine in one hand and the biggest bunch of flowers she'd ever seen in the other. 'I'm so sorry.'

He didn't wait for her to speak. He just stepped forward and put his arms around her. 'I should never have said anything. I'm sorry. I didn't mean any of it.'

She pushed him back a little. 'What? I've not to go and conquer the world? I've not to look at my career options and decide the best place I should be?'

He cringed. 'Well, yes. Yes, of course you should.' He held up the flowers and the wine again. 'But could we maybe discuss how we can still be friends, even if we're on different continents?'

She folded her arms across her chest. She didn't plan

on making this too easy. 'I thought you couldn't do that. I thought you weren't cut out for that?'

He held up the wine again. 'I'm hoping that maybe you could teach me. Maybe we could teach each other?'

There was a long silence. The clock ticked loudly in the distance.

She licked her lips. 'How about we go back a little? How about we drink the wine and let's take it from there?'

His sigh of relief was audible. She was prepared to give him a little leeway. But just a little. She still had to sort out in her head what she actually wanted to do.

He glanced at the table. 'Wow. Did you kill a tree?'

She groaned. 'I know. But I like to spread everything out in front of me. It makes it easier to compare.'

'Next you'll tell me you have a spreadsheet.'

Heat rushed into her cheeks and she turned the laptop around. 'Maybe.'

He held up the bottle. 'Should I open the wine?'

'I think you'll have to.'

She brought two glasses down from the cupboard while he uncorked the bottle. 'You don't mind doing this with me?'

He shook his head. 'What else am I going to do?'

She didn't know whether to be grateful or upset. His background knowledge of some of the bases would be invaluable. But she couldn't help but wonder how he felt about her considering going somewhere else.

It was the conversation that neither of them seemed able to have.

For the next hour he sat patiently next to her, filling her in on some of the details about the different bases she'd highlighted. It was mind-boggling. He could tell her about housing, facilities, airports. And if he didn't know something, he knew someone who did.

After an hour and a glass and a half of wine, Katsuko

sat back and sighed. Avery had an arm wrapped around her and she put her head on his shoulder. 'It's a lot to think about. I'll need to have a talk with Blake about making a base of preference request.'

Avery shifted in the seat beside her. 'When do you think you might do that?' His tone was a little strained.

She shuffled the papers in front of her. 'Whenever I've made up my mind. I'll need to give a few options. I want to make sure I choose carefully.'

He lifted his arm from her shoulder and leaned on the table. 'Have you spoken to Don?'

She pressed her lips together. It was a natural question. Her fingers slid up and down the stem of the wine glass. 'I spoke to him last week.'

'And?'

'He seemed to take it okay.'

'What about your grandmother?'

Her grip tightened on the glass. 'What about her?'

'Have you told her yet?'

She shook her head. 'I won't tell her until everything is final. She won't be happy. I know she won't. I'll need to try and make some other arrangements in case she argues with her carers again. I think I'll need to leave a deposit with another agency in case she refuses to let her carers in.'

'I thought she'd already worked her way around most of the local agencies?'

Katsuko sighed. Even though she knew it was true she was trying to push those thoughts from her head right now. Everywhere she looked it felt like there were barriers to her going. The guilt she felt about her grandmother. The guilt she felt about leaving Don after everything he'd done for her. The blossoming relationship she had with Avery. Was she really ready to give everything up?

The lump in her throat that had appeared a few seconds ago started to seem larger.

'Are you sure about this?'

Her reply was instantaneous. 'Don't you want me to go?'

There. She'd said it. The elephant in the room. She was finally calling him on this relationship. Finally asking what it meant.

Avery had a one-second look of panic. She could recognise it from a mile away. 'Of course I don't want you to go,' he replied. 'But if this is about your career, then I'd be a hypocrite not to support you. I've spent the last few years moving around in order to get the best experience that I could.'

She blinked. That didn't quite sound the way she wanted. 'What do you mean, *if this is about your career*? What else could it be about?'

He turned to face her. Darn it. Those pale green eyes were deadly serious. It made her stomach churn. She much preferred it when they had a wicked gleam in them, the one that usually led to…

'It could be about running away.'

'Running away from what?'

He bit his lip. He was obviously trying to find the right words. 'From the way your grandmother makes you feel. From the way other people make you feel.'

Her mouth instantly dried. 'My grandmother is just an old woman with old-fashioned views.'

'Your grandmother has never accepted you for who you are. Don't make excuses for her behaviour. By all accounts, she made your father uncomfortable, she's made Don uncomfortable and she's spent the last twenty-five years treating you as if you're not good enough. I actually think you're right to get away from her.'

She was stunned. And she hated the way those words made her feel.

'Then why are you saying anything?'

'Because I think you need to be clear about why you want to go.'

'What right do you have to comment? You're a fine one to talk about running away from family. You've spent the last few years doing it too.'

He nodded and pressed his hand against his chest. 'But I know why I distance myself from them. I don't want to be like them. I don't want to be like them at all.' He held up his hands. 'I see people in relationships here who look as if they'll stay together for ever. I have no examples of that in my family. I don't know what that is. I don't know if I'm even cut out for that.'

She held her breath. For a few seconds she'd been so annoyed about his words that she'd almost missed what he was telling her.

'And that's part of why you've moved so much?'

His eyes lowered. 'I've never really tried to find out. When it's time to leave a base I'm generally happy to. All relationships come to a natural end. I've never considered trying to maintain one when I've left.'

Her heart twisted in her chest. 'And that's what's going to happen to us?'

Was this his idea of letting her down gently? Because it felt like an elephant had just trampled across her chest. 'You're not prepared to even try?' She picked up the papers in front of her. 'So, if I decide to put in for a transfer, that's it? Goodbye, Katsuko?'

He opened his mouth to speak but nothing came out. He closed it again and swallowed. He looked at her steadily. 'What I think is that as soon as you tell your grandmother you're going, she'll make you feel guilty. I think you're making a really brave decision. And the best thing I can do is back you. I want you to feel happy and confident about where you decide to apply. I want you to know that you're a great nurse who'll probably get promoted six months after you leave here. I want you to know that you're good enough to go to any of these bases and they would be lucky to have you. You're making decisions about your life and your career, Katsuko. The last thing you want is for someone to stand in your way.'

She pressed her lips together. There was so much she wanted to say but she didn't want to make a fool of herself. What was the point of putting yourself out there, only to have it thrown back in your face?

She stared at the printouts for a minute. She was taking charge of her life. She'd thought she'd found something special. But maybe the connection she felt was all in her head?

I don't want you to stand in my way, Avery. I want you to stand by my side.

Those were the words she wanted to say—she just didn't have the courage to say them out loud.

She dug under the pile of papers and pulled out the one she'd left till last. 'We didn't talk about this one. What about this one? They put out a special call on Friday. There's only three weeks left if I want to request it.'

He paled visibly and reached for the paper. It was almost as if he was trying to choose his words carefully. 'Afghanistan. Why Afghanistan?'

She'd researched it until her brain had almost died from overload. 'The combat support hospital is more advanced that some modern inner-city ERs. They've devised more patented technology there than anywhere else in the world. The joint theatre hospital at one of the bases is renowned the world over. You should know. You've been there.'

It was almost like a challenge. He'd talked about nearly everywhere he'd been and even though he'd told her initially that he'd probably learned most in Afghanistan, he hadn't gone into the finer details.

He looked at her carefully. 'Why there? Why now?'

What was he asking her?

She couldn't have timed things any worse. It had taken her twenty-five years to find someone she could consider a future with, and as soon as she'd discovered that, she'd realised she had to spread her wings and fly if she wanted her career to develop. Apt for an air force nurse.

She licked her lips. None of the words she wanted to say seemed right. And some of the things he'd already said prickled more than they should. Was he right? Was she running away from things? And was she running away from him too?

'I think it will be good for me. I think it will give me the experience I need if I want my career to flourish.' It was the kind of answer you'd give to an interview question.

His face was unreadable. She had no idea what he was thinking. Her insides felt like they were dying. She wanted to tell him how much he meant to her. She wanted to tell him that she spent all day counting down the minutes until she could see him again. Wanted to tell him that she didn't even want to consider a future without him in it.

Her phone beeped and he picked it up from the table, frowned and handed it to her. It was her grandmother. Her fingers immediately started to punch out a reply but his hand closed over hers. 'Don't.'

The warmth of his hand sent pulses shooting up her arm. He was right there, right there in front of her but he didn't have his arms around her. He didn't have his lips on hers. The emptiness she felt right now was almost an ache.

'Why not?'

He squeezed his eyes closed for a second. 'How many times has she messaged you since she met me?'

The question took her by surprise but it didn't take much thought to answer. 'Every day.'

'And before that? Before that, how often did she message you?'

It hadn't even occurred to her. 'Maybe...once a week?'

He shook his head. 'She senses things, Katsuko. She senses the changes in you. She's still trying to control you. Once you tell her you want to leave she'll do everything she can to stand in your way.'

His clear green eyes were so intense, so sincere. And in a horrible way she knew he was right. She'd just been pushing things away, trying not to think about them too much.

'How much control you let her have over your life is up to you, Katsuko.'

His gaze was so intense, so penetrating that she had to look away.

All the words that couldn't be said.

She got that. She got that now.

This could be about them. Her grandmother was sensing change. She recognised the signs. She'd seen them in her daughter—and now she could see them in her granddaughter. Two women who had fallen in love. And in her grandmother's eyes with two totally unsuitable men.

She put her hand down on the table to steady her legs. Now she got why Avery wouldn't say the words.

If he felt the same way she did, he didn't want to make her choose. He wouldn't ask her to.

And he was right. As soon as she told her grandmother she'd requested to move base she'd be faced with a whole host of problems. Her phone would probably go non-stop.

She could almost see words forming on his lips. Avery—the confident, intelligent doctor she knew—was racked with self-doubt. His family history preyed on him in a way that it shouldn't. In a life without different bases, different career pathways, no grandmothers and no multi-married parents, she could see them sitting on a porch, growing old together.

Nothing in her head felt straight. How her grandmother continually made her feel. The fact that she hadn't spoken to Don about Afghanistan. How she would feel about being away from her family and friends for months at a time.

And the fact that right now she just wanted to love and be loved.

She felt herself start to tremble. This so wasn't like her. But she just didn't know what to say. She just didn't know what to think.

His gaze was fixed on her. It was like he was looking for a sign. Looking for a prompt so he could say what he really wanted to.

Tears pooled in her eyes. 'But she's my grandmother' was all that came out.

Avery looked at her for the longest time. Then he gave a little nod of his head. 'Yes. She is.' He brushed a kiss to the side of her cheek and walked out.

CHAPTER TEN

THE ALARM SHOT through the ER. A few newer members of staff frowned, trying to decipher why the cardiac arrest call sounded different.

The rest of the staff didn't hesitate. Katsuko lifted her small patient from the trolley and dropped to her knees. Blake's voice echoed on the Tannoy system.

'Drop! Cover! Hold!'

The shaking started a few seconds later.

Most of the staff here were old pros. They'd trained for this and had to use their training on a regular basis throughout the year. For the light quakes the alarm didn't sound. It only sounded for the moderate and strong quakes—anything above five on the Richter scale.

There was no space to get beneath the trolley so Katsuko pulled the little girl she'd been treating close to her chest and spoke quietly to her as the ground and walls shook around them.

There were inevitable noises. A few shrieks. A few crashes. The hospital was well prepared. Heavy items weren't stored on high shelves where they could fall and do harm. Larger pieces of furniture were bolted to walls—no one wanted a hospital wardrobe or filing cabinet to land on them.

The little girl didn't seem at all bothered. She'd just had her hand stitched after lacerating it on a piece of glass during a fall. Her mother had gone to the front desk to sign a few forms. Katsuko hoped that she had taken cover somewhere too.

Frank was in the room across the hall. He had an elderly patient next to him on the ground. 'You two okay?' he shouted.

She nodded, just as the trolley in his room managed to release its brake and roll towards them. 'Watch out!' she shouted.

Frank barely blinked as the shaking continued. He caught the trolley with one hand and one foot, protecting both himself and the patient.

He squinted up the clock in the hall. 'This one is lasting a bit longer than normal, isn't it?'

Katsuko nodded. 'Let's hope there's no damage.'

A phone cut through the shaking. It had a different tone from normal.

Frank mouthed a silent expletive at her as the force of the shaking started to diminish. They both knew exactly what phone that was. It meant there was a problem somewhere else in the hospital.

When the shaking finally stopped Katsuko jumped to her feet. Everything in her surrounding area seemed fine. She put her charge back on the trolley and pulled up the sides just as the mother reappeared. 'Is she okay?'

Katsuko nodded. 'We're both fine. How about you?'

The woman nodded, her trembling lip betraying her fear. 'Thank you.'

Katsuko glanced across the corridor. 'Need a hand, Frank?'

He shook his head as he snapped the brake back on the trolley and lifted his elderly patient easily on his own. She hid her smile. Health and Safety would have a fit.

Blake appeared at her side. 'Kat, ICU. Now. Two of the

ventilators are down and they need help bagging. The emergency generator hasn't kicked in.'

She took off at a run. Blake's voice carried behind her. 'Seiko, implement the phone muster. Frank, injury and patient reports. Lei, structural damage.'

They'd hear just how big the earthquake had been in a while, but in the meantime they had systems and processes in place to try and ensure the safety of all the staff and patients.

ICU was silently chaotic. She burst through the doors and was given an immediate wave by a member of staff in the corner. She ran straight over and took over bagging the patient. It wasn't a hard job—it was just essential to maintain the patient's breathing. The emergency generators usually kicked in straight away. This had never happened before.

Staff from other areas arrived too, all moving wherever needed. After a short while maintenance staff arrived, covered in dust, wheeling a portable generator alongside them.

'The line to the emergency generator has fractured. Repairs will take an hour. There's a gas leak somewhere else, so the main power can't be turned back on.'

The maintenance staff set up the portable generator and the staff from ICU connected the two ventilators. After a few minutes everything seemed to be working again. Katsuko was just putting down the bag and mask when Blake walked through the doors and waved her over.

The senior nurse shot her a glance. 'Thanks for your help.'

Katsuko gave her a nod and walked to the door. 'What's wrong?'

Blake looked anxious. He held open the door and started walking back along the corridor with her. 'Avery was due on duty. He isn't answering his house phone, his mobile or his page. Do you know where he could be?'

Katsuko shook her head. They'd parted on such bad terms last night that she no idea what his plans were for today. 'Are there reports of any problems?'

Blake nodded as they reached the ER front desk. 'Some reports are telling us already it was five point nine on the Richter scale. They also think we were only thirty miles away from the epicentre.'

'Are we expecting casualties?' She was asking the questions she should be asking. But not the questions she *wanted* to ask. She was on duty. She was a nurse. The military were expected to be able to react in the event of emergencies. All staff were supposed to respond.

Avery knew that. He'd been in emergency situations before. She couldn't understand why he wasn't here.

The emergency radio was on behind the desk, the Japanese voice speaking steadily. It sounded like there was some damage across the city. All of the modern buildings had been constructed to withstand earthquakes but some of the older buildings hadn't fared so well. It seemed that years of being shaken by earthquakes had caused some older foundations to finally crumble.

The emergency phone rang again and Blake answered. His brow furrowed as he listened intently. 'Yes, yes, no problem.'

He looked at the staff who had automatically collected around him—the emergency phone was almost like a homing beacon to ER staff. 'We're expecting between fifteen and twenty casualties, mainly broken bones and lacerations. There have been a number of wall collapses around us.' He replaced the receiver and glanced at Katsuko, muttering under his breath, 'Where on earth can he be? We could use him right now.'

The deep voice came from behind her. 'Who could you use?'

Katsuko jumped and spun around. She hadn't expected

to see Don here. She thought he'd be coordinating everything from the control centre.

Blake gave him a nod. 'General Williams. We're missing Dr Flynn from the staff muster. Can't raise him at all. We don't know where he is.'

'I know where he is.' He touched Katsuko's elbow and pulled her to the side.

'What? How do you know where Avery is?'

She didn't understand. Don and Avery hadn't even had an official introduction yet. She hadn't meant to keep him away from Don, it had just worked out that way.

Don spoke in a low voice. 'Avery came to see me earlier.'

'What? Why would he do that?' Now she was totally confused. Why on earth would he go to see Don?

Don sighed. 'He wanted to meet me. He wanted to tell me that he might have upset my daughter by not telling her how he felt about her. He also told me that he didn't want to stand in the way of your career plans.'

'Why on earth would he tell you any of that?' She didn't get it. She really didn't get it. Last night all she'd wanted him to do was tell her how he felt about her—to be honest with her. He hadn't seemed able to do it, but he could tell Don instead?

Don laid a hand on her arm. 'He went to see Hiroko.'

'What? Why?' This was just getting crazier by the minute.

'He felt as if she might try and ruin your plans. He didn't want her to do that. He told me he was going to see her and tell her how great a nurse you were, how great your career prospects could be, and…' he paused '…how proud she should be of you.'

Katsuko gulped. That didn't sound like the actions of a man who didn't care about her. 'Why would he do that?' she whispered.

Don looked at her with the patient eyes of a father. 'He

also wanted to tell her that at some point he intended to propose to you. And that as your husband he wouldn't allow his wife—or your future children—to be treated as if they weren't good enough.' Don gave a little smile. 'It seems he's got the size of your grandmother.'

Katsuko looked around. 'Then where is he?'

Don took a deep breath. 'That's why I'm here. I can't raise Hiroko on the phone. I've heard reports that some of the houses in the area have collapsed.'

'What?' She stepped backwards, reaching out for the wall behind her to steady herself.

Don nodded. 'There's a military car and driver outside.' He glanced over at Blake, who was hovering around, pretending he wasn't listening. 'We've called in all the extra staff. I'm sure you can be spared.'

Blake walked over to a nearby cupboard and pulled out an emergency pack and hard hat. 'Here. Take these with you. And bring Avery back. I need him. I need you both.'

Katsuko flung her hands around Don's neck. 'Thank you,' she whispered.

'Stay safe,' he replied as he handed her a radio. 'Let me know how you are.'

It took more than an hour to reach her grandmother's street. Some roads had wide fractures in them, meaning traffic couldn't go the normal routes. Potholes had opened in some places, with a whole variety of police cordons around trees or buildings affected by the earthquake.

Her grandmother lived in a more rural part of Tokyo. The houses were older single-storey wooden constructions with thatched roofs.

At least they used to be.

Two out of the four houses on the street were still standing.

The other two had collapsed completely, leaving their thatched roofs on what resembled piles of firewood.

'That one!' said Katsuko, and the driver ground to a halt.

She jumped from the car and ran towards the rubble. A few people were at the other collapsed house in the street, picking up strewn belongings.

Katsuko felt a wave of panic wash over her. Where did she even start? Was her grandmother in there? Was Avery?

She tried to be logical, tried to think with her head instead of her heart.

She crouched down and looked at the pile in front of her. The driver appeared at her side, bent down and unwound her tightly gripped fingers from the radio.

The radio. Of course. So much for thinking with her head. She heard him talking rapidly. All she could think right now was whether anyone could be alive in there.

'Avery! Avery,' she started shouting. Apart from the noise of distant sirens, the street was strangely quiet.

'Sobo! Sobo!' The Japanese word for grandmother was usually an affectionate term. It had never really fitted her grandmother—even now it felt strange to use it.

She shuddered. The house looked so alien to her—as if a giant had walked along the street and flattened it with his foot. It was odd, though, parts of the thatched roof looked strangely intact—as if a crane could come along and lift it back up on top of a newly constructed house.

She started to pull at some of the shattered wood, throwing it behind her as she tried to see anything she recognised amongst the debris.

The driver joined her. 'What did they say?' she asked.

His face was serious. 'I've got to radio back if there are any sign of survivors. Emergency services are only reacting to reports of trapped survivors right now.'

Of course they were. What he wasn't saying out loud

was that the emergency services didn't have the resources right now to recover bodies. That would come later.

She started to work more frantically, her muscles burning as she tossed pieces of wood behind her.

After ten minutes the driver touched her elbow, almost earning himself a piece of wood in the face. 'Listen.'

She froze, her ears pricking up instantly.

There it was. A kind of moan.

She dropped to her knees. 'Avery! *Sobo!* Hiroko!' she shouted at the pile of rubble.

There it was again. A faint noise in the debris.

The driver knelt beside her. They practically had their ears to the ground.

'Avery!' she shouted again.

'Kat.' It wasn't a shout. It was more like a hoarse whisper.

She started pulling at the wood again, trying to get closer to the source of his voice. After a few minutes she realised it was useless. The edge of the roof stopped her going any further.

She leaned in, pressing her face right up against the thatch of the roof. She didn't care about the fact it was scratching her face. She didn't care about anything other than finding out that the people she loved were actually in there.

'Avery, are you there? Are you okay?'

There was a bit of a groan. Then a quip, 'Oh, so you're talking to me now.'

A tear slid down her cheek. He was alive. He was definitely alive.

She tried to find some words. 'Are you okay?' she repeated. 'What about my grandmother?'

It took a few seconds to get a reply. Was he going in and out of consciousness? Could he have a head injury?

'Give me a minute.'

The driver pressed on her shoulder. He was back on the phone, obviously trying to get them some assistance in the midst of chaos.

It was too quiet. She could hardly bear it. 'Avery?'

She adjusted her position, trying to figure out exactly where he was. It wasn't easy and she ended up crawling over part of the roof. 'Avery?'

'I've got her.'

'You have?' A second wave of relief washed over her. 'Is she okay?'

'I think so.' He made another strange noise. 'I'm trapped next to her. Give me a second.'

The waiting game. The thing she really wasn't good at.

'She's breathing. I'm just trying to wake her up.'

Katsuko was conscious of the driver talking next to her in rapid Japanese. He took off down the road towards some of the bewildered-looking neighbours who were standing in the middle of the street, staring at the road.

'Oh, now she's awake. She's glaring at me again.'

Katsuko started babbling in Japanese, telling her grandmother that she was here and she would get her out. Telling her to be strong.

She heard a rapid string of Japanese but it was so quietly spoken she couldn't make out a word.

'Avery, what's she saying?'

Avery could hardly move. His legs and chest were pinned. The only thing he could really move was his head and one of his arms.

One minute he'd been standing in the doorway, having an almost argument with Katsuko's grandmother, the next minute the ground had rumbled all around them and the house had started to shake. His brain had screamed at them to get out of there.

But Hiroko had been in her wheelchair and the handles

hadn't been facing him. As he'd tried to jump inside to get her out something had crashed into his back and knocked them both to the ground. He didn't remember much after that.

He tried to take a deep breath. Impossible. Breathing was a struggle. He was guessing that one of his lungs might have collapsed. He only hoped it was a pneumothorax and not a haemothorax. It wouldn't do it have a medical emergency right now. He didn't want to think where he could be bleeding from.

Katsuko kept talking. Nervous energy. He could only imagine how frustrated she was right now.

Hiroko started another tirade and he aimed the pen torch at her. One of his legs was pinned under her wheelchair, the other caught between part of the roof and the floor. She had a large wound on her head, but her temperament and voice remained unchanged. It was amazing. It was almost as if he could understand every word she was spitting at him. Hatred was a pretty universal language.

'Avery, what's she saying? I can't hear her.'

'I think she's telling me she doesn't like me much.'

Silence for a second. It was clear Katsuko was trying to make sense of what was going on. 'Why on earth were you visiting my grandmother?'

He let his head rest back on the floor. This was so not how he wanted to do this.

He'd spoken to the General. Or, he should say, he'd been interrogated by the General. Don Williams was an impressive man. It was clear that for him, without any question, Katsuko was his daughter. Genes didn't matter. Blood didn't matter.

By the time Avery had told him how he felt about his daughter and what he intended to do, he'd felt lucky to finally leave with the General's blessing.

He reached over and touched Hiroko's shoulder. It was

all he could do. His pen torch was the only light they had—thank goodness he'd had it in his back pocket. 'Hiroko, I don't know how long we will be here. Katsuko's outside, she knows we're trapped, she'll get help.' He tried to wriggle a little bit to ease the pressure on his right hip.

In theory, Hiroko shouldn't be able to understand a word he was saying. But he saw something flash across her eyes—just like he had the first time he'd met her—and just like he had when he'd arrived today and told her how much he loved her granddaughter. He turned the pen torch to look at the time on his watch. Really? How long had he been unconscious?

Then something else occurred to him. How long had Hiroko lain trapped in the dark, wondering if anyone would come to rescue her? She must have been terrified.

He wriggled some more and lifted his hand from Hiroko's shoulder and moved it down, taking her gnarled hand in his.

She made a little noise of displeasure but she didn't let go.

'Avery?' Katsuko's voice was just to his right. It didn't seem so far away now. There was only this roof separating them. How long before he could look into those dark brown eyes again?

He took a deep breath. 'I came to tell your grandmother how special I thought you were. I came to tell her that you might have to move base. You're in the air force, it's expected of you.'

There was a sniff beside him. And he knew instantly what it was. A silent tear slid down Hiroko's face and he gently squeezed her gnarled hand.

Katsuko hadn't answered. She'd realised that he hadn't told her grandmother that she was choosing to go away, choosing to find a new life. He'd made it sound like it was part of her air force medical corps service.

He heard some discussion through the thatch, but it was all in Japanese, he couldn't understand a word.

'Avery? I've got an axe.'

'What?' He couldn't help but shout his reply.

'I have to do something. It will be hours before we can get help. There's been a few older buildings that have collapsed across the city. But most of the damage is to the streets. We're going to try and get through the thatch. We need to get some air to you. Even if we can't get you out, we can maybe get some water to you both.'

Air. He hadn't really thought about air. Wouldn't some just come through the densely packed thatch? In truth, he had no idea. 'I'm not sure about this. I don't really want an axe in the head.'

'We'll do it to the side. I can't stand here and do nothing. We have to try and reach you.'

'Have you any idea how thick this thatch is?'

'I guess we're about to find out.'

She shouted some more instructions, asking questions and trying to find out their positions under the thatch.

Eventually, after a lot more discussion outside, he heard the noise of the axe. It took a long, long time. At first the noise seemed far away. It took quite a time before the actual vibrations of the axe started to reach them. Their judgement was good. It sounded close enough but not so close as to do them any harm. The light started to filter through as some of the thatch was dragged away. Eventually, a metre away from his head they finally broke through.

For a few seconds all he could see were hands, pulling and pulling at the thatch to try and make a gap. It wasn't large, certainly not big enough to get through, but the light and warm air that flooded in was welcome.

A few seconds later somebody shone a torch inside. Katsuko started shouting first in Japanese, then in English.

'Avery! Avery! I can see you.' Her hand reached in, her fingertips barely touching the top of his hair.

It didn't matter. It was enough.

The torch light swung slightly past him and she spoke rapidly to her grandmother, obviously trying to reassure her. He waited for the venom, the disapproving answer, but it didn't come. Her hand was still in his, and he gave it a little squeeze again. This time she squeezed back.

'You have no idea how glad I am to see you. I was so scared. So worried about you both.' Katsuko took a deep breath. 'I'm so glad you were here with my grandmother.'

It didn't matter how long they'd been here. It didn't matter how uncomfortable they were. It didn't matter that his breathing was awkward. All he cared about was the fact that she'd come. The fact that she was here.

She pushed in a bottle of water, it was tied to a stick this time and his hand could reach it. It took a minute to open the top with one hand, then hold it towards Hiroko to let her have a drink. Of course he spilled it half over her. But she didn't complain. She just closed her eyes in grateful silence.

Katsuko's face pressed up to the space again. Her cheek was smeared with dust and her normally smooth hair was sticking up in all directions. He'd never seen anyone quite so beautiful.

'When I get you out of here, you and I need to talk about you coming to see my grandmother.' The fearful tone had left her voice. She was still anxious, but now she could actually see them both she obviously felt a bit more reassured.

'Your grandmother and I have reached an understanding,' he replied.

'What? What do you mean?'

He smiled as he craned his neck to turn his face towards her. 'I've been taking lessons.'

'Lessons in what?'

He held her gaze. He'd been practising and practising

over in his head. He wanted to get it just right. 'This isn't exactly how I wanted to say this. But it's important. Probably the most important thing I'll ever say.' He concentrated hard. *'Kokoro no sokokara aishiteru.'*

There was a little gasp. 'What did you just say?'

'Kokoro no sokokara aishiteru.' This time he had more confidence. This time he followed it with something new. *'Aishiteru.'*

She didn't speak. She didn't say anything.

'Katsuko Williams, you have my heart. I love you. Last night I thought if I told you that, I'd be standing in your way. And I don't ever want to stand in your way. I want to stand by your side. You're unsettled. You think you don't fit anywhere. But I know where you fit. You fit with me. You are my perfect fit.' He stopped for a breath. The pain in his lung was constant but it wouldn't stop him from saying what he needed to say. 'I wanted to say this when I had my arms around you, not when we've been pushed apart. So get us out of here soon, so I can say it again. *Aishiteru.* I love you.'

Katsuko started sobbing. 'You tell me now? You tell me like this?'

'I've spent so much time wondering if I can be what you need. I've never been somewhere I don't want to leave. I've never been with someone I don't want to leave. But you're perfect for me. I want to make this work. I want to do anything at all to make this work. I love you, Katsuko, and get used to hearing it because I can say it in two languages now.'

'Avery Flynn, you are the most annoying man I've ever met.'

His heart skipped a beat, then she continued, 'And the most adorable. And the most infuriating. That kiss. That kiss in the middle of Hachiko Crossing. It blew my mind. I couldn't think straight. I haven't thought straight ever since. I want to be kissed like that every day for the rest of my life.'

'And I want to be the man to do that.'

Something shook around them. Avery frowned. 'What's that?'

It happened again. And again. Then again.

Her face pressed back up at the hole. 'It's me,' said Katsuko. 'I'm getting you out of there. I need to be kissed again and I don't want to wait.' He heard her shout in Japanese to the others and the thudding intensified. He turned towards Hiroko. Tears were streaming down her face.

'Hiroko? Are you okay? Are you in pain?'

She shook her head. 'No.'

He blinked. She'd just answered in English. Was he hallucinating? Maybe his oxygen level was lower than it should be.

'I love her,' he said. 'I promise you I'll take good care of her. I know you don't want her to marry an American. I know you didn't want your daughter to marry an American. But Katsuko is the woman for me.' He gave her a smile. 'She has my heart.'

Hiroko didn't speak. She just gave him a gracious nod.

A hand broke in and grabbed his shoulder. 'Come on,' shouted Katsuko. 'Hold on, honey. Not long now.'

He was almost relieved when the pounding stopped. The rescuers were too close to use the axe now. But they seemed to use every other tool they could find to try and break the thatch apart to get to them. More and more hands appeared, pulling at the edges of the thatch and doing their best to break it apart. It was tough. Avery could see that. Something that had lasted this long didn't want to give up now.

Finally there were arms around his shoulders. Katsuko let out a shriek. 'Avery? What's wrong? You're hurt. Why didn't you tell me?' He winced as her hand came into contact with his side and came up smeared in red. He sucked in a breath and she must have noticed his uneven breathing straight away. 'You have a pneumothorax?' She signalled to the driver as she pulled at his shirt. 'Get the rest of this thatch away. I need to check him over and get him out of here,' she shouted to the rescuers.

She stopped for a second and turned her attention to her grandmother, speaking to her in a low voice in Japanese and examining her as best she could.

He couldn't help but smile. This was her—the woman he loved. Taking charge. Her emergency skills shone through. She would excel in Afghanistan and he would be right by her side.

When she came back to him he whispered in her ear, 'You'd better have pressed send on that application because I pressed send last night.'

She pulled back, her eyes wide. 'You did?'

'Of course I did. Do you know how many guys will love you over there?'

She raised her eyebrows. 'But I'm only interested in one guy. The thing is, he can't get over his family history. He doesn't seem to know that he and I can make our own history.'

An oxygen canister appeared from somewhere and Katsuko slid the mask over his face. He pulled it aside. 'You have your work cut out for you. I might be a slow learner but someone in my family has got to set a good example. I figure it should be me.'

He slid his hand into hers. '*Kokoro no sokokara aishiteru.* I'd like to have our own saying. How about always and for ever? How does that sound?'

Her brown eyes met his and she put a hand on either side of his head as she leaned in to kiss him. 'That sounds perfect.'

EPILOGUE

THE BRIDE AND groom had decided to come back to Tokyo to get married. Hiroko was too frail to travel and Katsuko wouldn't get married without Don being there to give her away.

Avery had reluctantly invited his parents with their new partners, and his sister with her new baby. 'Don't worry,' promised Katsuko with a wink. 'Any one of them gets out of order, the new Mrs Flynn will deal with them.'

Avery couldn't be prouder. His bride, in a bright red gown, was stunning. They'd returned from Afghanistan a captain and a major. Katsuko had blossomed in the intense environment. Next stop was the San Antonio Military Medical Center, the biggest and most advanced military hospital in the US.

He lifted the glass of champagne to the room filled with their family and friends. 'I'd like everyone to raise their glasses with me. I want you all to raise a glass to the man sitting in the corner of the room—a man most of you won't know.' He gave a nod of his head. 'This, ladies and gentlemen, is Dwayne Cooper. Dr Dwayne Cooper, who was supposed to take up his posting eighteen months ago in Okatu, Japan. Dwayne, however, had other ideas and decided to come down with malaria instead, meaning—with one day's notice—I was the one who climbed on that plane at Hill

Air Force base. I had no idea what would lie ahead. I had no idea I'd meet the love of my life and find a woman that I'd want to spend the rest of my life with.'

Katsuko was beaming. Don was sitting beside her in his dress uniform and couldn't look prouder. Her grandmother was next to Avery and had shed a tear during the ceremony.

Katsuko stood from her seat and wrapped her arms around his neck, kissing him on the lips. She lifted up her champagne glass from the table and showed it to the guests. 'To Dr Dwayne Cooper. My colleagues tell me that you're wonderful to work with, but you'll forgive me if I have a bias towards Major Flynn.'

The guests laughed and sipped their champagne.

Avery slipped his arm around his wife's waist. The wedding dinner had run later than expected and the hotel's full-length windows showed the dark sky outside. He lifted his glass again. 'One more thing, most of you will know my wife's nickname. So join me, everyone, in raising your glasses to my own *faiyakuraka*—Captain Katsuko Flynn.'

He gave a little signal to someone and a few seconds later the sky lit up with fireworks behind them.

Her eyes widened as she turned towards him and put both hands on his shoulders. 'You got me fireworks?'

'Of course I got you fireworks,' he bent to whisper in her ear. 'Now, how about we re-enact Hachiko Crossing?'

She grinned at him. 'I can't think of anything I want to do more.'

And so they did.

As the multi-coloured fireworks streaked across the sky and the guests cheered.

* * * * *

If you enjoyed this story, check out these other great reads from Scarlet Wilson

THE DOCTOR'S BABY SECRET
A TOUCH OF CHRISTMAS MAGIC
THE DOCTOR SHE LEFT BEHIND
CHRISTMAS WITH THE MAVERICK MILLIONAIRE

All available now!

MILLS & BOON®

Hardback – October 2016

ROMANCE

The Return of the Di Sione Wife	Caitlin Crews
Baby of His Revenge	Jennie Lucas
The Spaniard's Pregnant Bride	Maisey Yates
A Cinderella for the Greek	Julia James
Married for the Tycoon's Empire	Abby Green
Indebted to Moreno	Kate Walker
A Deal with Alejandro	Maya Blake
Surrendering to the Italian's Command	Kim Lawrence
Surrendering to the Italian's Command	Kim Lawrence
A Mistletoe Kiss with the Boss	Susan Meier
A Countess for Christmas	Christy McKellen
Her Festive Baby Bombshell	Jennifer Faye
The Unexpected Holiday Gift	Sophie Pembroke
Waking Up to Dr Gorgeous	Emily Forbes
Swept Away by the Seductive Stranger	Amy Andrews
One Kiss in Tokyo...	Scarlet Wilson
The Courage to Love Her Army Doc	Karin Baine
Reawakened by the Surgeon's Touch	Jennifer Taylor
Second Chance with Lord Branscombe	Joanna Neil
The Pregnancy Proposition	Andrea Laurence
His Illegitimate Heir	Sarah M. Anderson

0916 GEN STD HB

MILLS & BOON®

Large Print – October 2016

ROMANCE

Wallflower, Widow...Wife!	Ann Lethbridge
Bought for the Greek's Revenge	Lynne Graham
An Heir to Make a Marriage	Abby Green
The Greek's Nine-Month Redemption	Maisey Yates
Expecting a Royal Scandal	Caitlin Crews
Return of the Untamed Billionaire	Carol Marinelli
Signed Over to Santino	Maya Blake
Wedded, Bedded, Betrayed	Michelle Smart
The Greek's Nine-Month Surprise	Jennifer Faye
A Baby to Save Their Marriage	Scarlet Wilson
Stranded with Her Rescuer	Nikki Logan
Expecting the Fellani Heir	Lucy Gordon

HISTORICAL

The Many Sins of Cris de Feaux	Louise Allen
Scandal at the Midsummer Ball	Marguerite Kaye & Bronwyn Scott
Marriage Made in Hope	Sophia James
The Highland Laird's Bride	Nicole Locke
An Unsuitable Duchess	Laurie Benson

MEDICAL

Seduced by the Heart Surgeon	Carol Marinelli
Falling for the Single Dad	Emily Forbes
The Fling That Changed Everything	Alison Roberts
A Child to Open Their Hearts	Marion Lennox
The Greek Doctor's Secret Son	Jennifer Taylor
Caught in a Storm of Passion	Lucy Ryder

MILLS & BOON®

Hardback – November 2016

ROMANCE

Di Sione's Virgin Mistress	Sharon Kendrick
Snowbound with His Innocent Temptation	Cathy Williams
The Italian's Christmas Child	Lynne Graham
A Diamond for Del Rio's Housekeeper	Susan Stephens
Claiming His Christmas Consequence	Michelle Smart
One Night with Gael	Maya Blake
Married for the Italian's Heir	Rachael Thomas
Unwrapping His Convenient Fiancée	Melanie Milburne
Christmas Baby for the Princess	Barbara Wallace
Greek Tycoon's Mistletoe Proposal	Kandy Shepherd
The Billionaire's Prize	Rebecca Winters
The Earl's Snow-Kissed Proposal	Nina Milne
The Nurse's Christmas Gift	Tina Beckett
The Midwife's Pregnancy Miracle	Kate Hardy
Their First Family Christmas	Alison Roberts
The Nightshift Before Christmas	Annie O'Neil
It Started at Christmas...	Janice Lynn
Unwrapped by the Duke	Amy Ruttan
Hold Me, Cowboy	Maisey Yates
Holiday Baby Scandal	Jules Bennett

1016 GEN STD HB